Chung Piece

A Novel

D1176563

Copyright © 2020 by James Rose

All rights reserved.

This novel's story and characters are fictitious. Certain long-established institutions are mentioned, but the characters involved in them are wholly imaginary.

It's about what you do with what you know

Gar Walker

It's been a few months since I saddled up, hauled ass out of Aspen. Considering the state of the world, and I where now find myself, no harm in going back to my daily ritual of journaling. Lots has happened since my narrow escape from the Roaring Fork Valley. I ended up driving as far south as Big Bend on the Texas-Mexico border. Ruminating over my forced departure among the Chisos Mountains, Texas madrone and Arizona cypress. Waking each morning to the song of Santa Elena canyon wren. I camped for weeks on the banks of the Rio Grande; going into Terlingua whenever necessary to buy food, water, life's essentials.

My contracting the corona virus occurred on one of those trips into town. I don't know how or when but my guess is from sharing a pitcher of sangria one night at a bar with a couple Aussie girls. They were visiting from Marfa before returning to Austin and then home to Fremantle. It was the worst flu I've ever had. My sense of smell and taste, gone. I could hardly breath. It took three weeks for me to come out the other side. I had to deal with the virus in a campsite. I was never tested, but reading the news, talking to a Terlingua nurse, my symptoms were obvious of the virus that has dropped our world to its knees. Once I started feeling better by early March, my time camping was over. I needed a bed and sheets. I'd lost twenty pounds. But where to go now?

October

My first assignment working as a freelancer for the Aspen Herald was to report a story for the crime beat involving a house break-in. Last weekend, late Saturday night. I was given the story first thing Monday morning.

"Quick story," said Beau Norman, my new editor. "Call the sheriff's office, give me two-hundred fifty words by five tonight."

Well, it's now Thursday of the following week. I have yet to file. Norman is not happy about my missed deadline. We had a private meeting about it earlier today.

"Unacceptable," he said, as I closed his office door behind me. He was sitting behind a big mahogany desk. "We take deadlines serious here. You understand?" Of course I understood. I apologized. "At least give me your excuse," he said.

My excuse to Norman was the story within the last week had unfolded into something unexpected. The upshot is a South Korean tourist named Won Seok Chung travelled to Aspen the same week of my own arrival. On his second day in town, Chung broke into a palatial Red Mountain house which he thought belonged to Carlyle Erikson, a distinguished journalist from New York and current chair of the Roaring Fork Institute. Erikson was not home because the house was not his. Chung picked the wrong one. When questioned by the police after first running from the scene but then returning forty-five minutes later, in broken English, he cited "voices of demons" in his head that told him to proceed with the break-in.

I am a reporter and I report on what was said and that is what was said. Tom Wolfe said the world in front of us is the best source for compelling fiction. I think he's right. The explanation Chung gave was the kicker. The South Korean government is now involved in the case.

"So you see Mr. Norman, with each passing day the story gets more and more complicated." Norman twirled his pen, narrowed his eyes. I was being vetted.

Finally: "You know Meko, we were all sad to see Jack go."

"I'm sure you were, he's a great journ—"

"You know what he said about you?"

"Can't say I do."

"Great writer, outgoing, smart, ambitious..."

"Kind of him."

"And when I read the clips you sent, I must say I was impressed."

"Thank you, Mr. Norman."

"But that's not why I hired you to freelance."

"No?"

"No. You know why I hired you? Jack said you never miss your deadlines. That's why I hired you." I cleared my throat.

"But here we are and you're already days late on one of your first stories. Now, I know Jack to be an honest guy. But—"

"I am really sorry Mr. Norman. It's just that I think there's more to this story. I think there's something bigger going on here."

"Bigger?"

"Yeah, bigger."

"And what makes you say that?"

"Can't really say. More just a...hunch."

Norman laughed. "Meko, whether there is something bigger happening, a deadline's a deadline."

"Yes, yes of course."

"I'm about to turn seventy-two. I should be retired, but I'm not. You know why? I love this job. I'm from the old school where missed deadlines aren't tolerated. You miss anymore, you're toast. Understand?"

"Yes, Mr. Norman, I understand."

"Good. Anyway, whatever it is you've reported so far, give me a summary of the ordeal tomorrow. I'll even run it at five hundred words...if you have enough material."

"Oh I do Mr. Norman, thank you and I won't let it happen again."

"Good. Now, before you go, know that you can keep working this story. Just because we put something out, doesn't mean it's over. But I don't need to tell you that, right?"

"No, sir."

"Keep at it if you think there's more under the hood. The shit that goes on in this town…"

"Thank you sir."

"One last thing. I want you to meet another new employee we have joining us."

"Sure, anytime."

"Her name's Alyssa. Young like you. She's working for us as a free-lance photographer."

"She here?"

"Should be. Talk to Marlene at the front, she'll know. Anyway, I want you using Alyssa whenever possible. The photos from your clips aren't bad. I want to make sure Alyssa is being used. She's very talented. Got it?"

"Copy. Alyssa. Photographer."

"Good. Oh, there's one more thing. I want us to meet again soon and talk about your goals. Not in the office. Over beers. Sound good? I want to help you, Meko. My hunch is you're not here in Aspen just to party. Or maybe you are? Anyway…till next time."

I found Marlene at her desk. She was on the phone and I waited until she was finished.

"Hey Marlene, it's Meko Torres, the new guy…we met last week?"

"Hey Meko, what can I do for ya?"

"Norman wanted me to meet another new employee. Alyssa? You know if she's here or not?"

"Just missed her. Left about ten minutes ago to go shoot. You want I can give you her contact?"

"Sure, thanks Marlene."

"Anytime."

Outside the Herald office, I tried calling Carlyle Erikson. Again, no answer. I am trying to talk to as many different sources as possible including Erikson, but he has routinely neglected picking up his phone despite our agreed upon times. Not everyone likes to talk to reporters, I understand that, but for Erikson to continually not hold up his side of the agreement? Prick. Perhaps there is more to the story on his end, who knows. All I need from him is one decent quote and I will be happy. Norman told me when he assigned the story that he didn't think Erikson would talk but if so, "bueno."

I am new here and want to make a good impression with regards to my skills in tracking people down and writing balanced, well-rounded stories. I thought it a minor coup when, with the permission of Pitkin County sheriff Shane Bledsoe, I was able to speak however briefly with Chung himself. He is being held in the Pitkin County jail and for most of the questions I asked in my five minutes of allotted time, he said "no comment." But when I asked him why he came to Aspen in the first place, his eyes lit up and with excitement he said one word: "extreme." I didn't know what he meant but later I found out that he became obsessed in recent years with a movie called Aspen Extreme. The movie played, oddly, on Korean cable television one night while Chung was at work.

Chung comes from a wealthy South Korean oil family. He is a vice president, something for the Korean state oil company who bought out his grandfather's private oil business for many millions years ago. Terms of the deal were such that his twenty year old grandson was to be hired and to have the words 'vice president' included in his title. Didn't matter what he did. Grandpa, sensitive to the optics of the Chung family legacy in Korean energy. The state oil company signed the agreement. Won Seok Chung got a job, title, but no responsibility. All hat, no cattle as they say in ranching.

Toiling away at his desk late one night after a boozy dinner with his ex-wife asking for his signature on a new Mercedes lease agreement, he flicked on his office television to see scenes of skiing in a place called

Aspen. Won Seok was transfixed. Blue sky, snowy slopes, pretty girls and a story line involving two ski instructor buddies new to Aspen from Detroit. Before watching the film that night, Chung had no clue Aspen even existed. After, he went down the rabbit hole on reading everything about the town's history and the colourful characters that have called the mountain town at almost eight thousand feet home. All of that back story won't be in my story for this weekend's paper. It will be a much more boring account of what happened that night and the international legal implications of Won Seok Chung's crime.

Three weeks ago, I moved to Aspen driving north from my hometown of Arroyo Seco, New Mexico. I've moved a lot in my twenties. Writing this journal keeps me grounded. From New Mexico, I was captivated by the drive over Independence Pass to reach the Roaring Fork Valley. The pass closes for the season at the end of October through May. The steep, windy road crosses many avalanche paths. The amount of work to keep it clear and safe is too much for Colorado's Department of Transportation. It is a wonderfully scenic drive though the Sawatch Rocky Mountains and while driving I couldn't help but spot several desirous locations for backcountry skiing. Too bad the state doesn't maintain the road over what used to be called Hunter Pass through the winter months. Instead of eight hours when the pass is closed, the drive was only five though I extended it by detouring west before crossing the border to hike around O'Keeffe's old ranch near Abiquiu. Fine countryside everyone should visit.

I've been assigned other stories as well but they've all been little two-hundred word event advancers. Fundraisers, ski swaps and so forth. I am not above that type of work and I was pleased to see my first story published on the last page last week. The byline read: "Meko Torrez." I was pissed to see my last name spelt with a 'z' instead of an 's'. I am proud of my lineage and demanded Norman to make the correction for future stories. I am fourteenth generation New Mexican. My family is a confusing mix of Spanish, Mexican, and Tiwa Indian. It is near impossible, so I have been told, to know how much of what I am. What I do know is that I have jet black wavy hair and a perma-tan complexion.

Sometimes in bars I'm called "chief" by drunken white guys. But the same has also occurred with (drunken) girls that I am attracted to and who are attracted to me. The girls that I am thinking of all end up saying that I have hair like the Canadian Prime Minister "only better, chief." I have no clue who they are talking about but I'll take it. In Arroyo Seco, lots of people look like me. Of my appearance, I never thought anything of it. Not until I moved to New Hampshire to study at Dartmouth on a ski racing scholarship. Taos Ski Valley is fifteen minutes up the road from Arroyo Seco and it is where I learned to ski fast. I was fortunate the now dying sport opened doors for me to places like Dartmouth.

In Hanover, most people never knew my actual name. My handle became "chief" or "Torres of Taos" from the first week of school all the way to cap and gown. Whether "chief" was meant to be derogatory, I don't know. I didn't mind being called either because they both came from my fitness coach on the ski team who I adored then, and still do to this day. Fitz was one of those old school disciplinarians that are a dying breed in this age of helicopter parenting and politically correct teaching pedagogy. He was fired last year for shouting swearwords at freshman athletes. It still makes me angry to think of how that all happened.

The name Meko comes from my Tiwa lineage. A great grandfather on my dad's side was a chief of the Taos Pueblo and his name was Meko Concha. My father was killed in the Gulf War and I was raised as an only child by my mother who runs an art gallery to this day in Taos' central plaza. Her Spanish great-grandfather owned lots of dirt in the Taos townsite and also several sections of ranching land around Arroyo Seco. The Taos airport was developed on some of his land and he made a few bucks selling it to the people concerned with having an airport way back when. Some of his land is still held in the family but, according to my mother, is behind impenetrable trusts inaccessible to anyone.

The gallery my mother owns is in a building owned by the family. It used to be, as she likes to tell her tourist clients, the location of an infamous bar frequented often by people like DH Lawrence when he used to call Taos home. I am proud of my mother and I like her choice of artists represented. They push boundaries with their work. The pieces hung on the gallery's walls I think is meant solely to distinguish the identity of Taos art from the usual oil landscapes of the surrounding countryside and scenes of the Pueblo. Not that there is anything wrong with that kind of work. I could look at Jerry Jordan's pictures from dawn to dusk. Same with Jim Wagner. But I agree "diversifying the market" as some dealers would say, is good for Taos' reputation.

In my spare time, I explore Aspen's surrounding Elk Mountains with their countless groves of golden leafed Aspen trees. Fall colours are showing. Soon, the leaves will all be on the forest floor and I am eager to hike to the many different lakes before they are. I need to get a lay of this land that I now call home. I only decided to move here because my old college buddy Jack Badenhausen said he could use some help with the Herald of which he was the assistant editor under Norman. In between him reaching out and me arriving here, he returned to his old job in California writing about music for the Los Angeles Times. Better money.

Anyway, I was ready to make a change from writing for the Taos newspaper for the past year whose depressingly small and shrinking budget could by summer's end only afford a town council reporter. Nothing more, and not for me. My girlfriend wanted us to settle down and buy a house. She wanted commitment and babies and me mowing our mortgaged front lawn every Saturday morning. I felt the walls closing in. I needed out. In Aspen, I saw another fresh start. Greener grass. Despite having a boujee reputation unlike anywhere else I'd lived. An opportunity to help a friend, see a new area and maybe meet my future wife. Maybe make a few bucks teaching skiing on the side. I don't want to commit to settling down. Not yet. What a frightening concept.

I graduated Dartmouth with an art history degree six years ago. Since then, I have incessantly moved around the United States. I've worked mainly as a reporter for community newspapers but also the occasional winter as a part-time ski instructor. I no longer am involved at all with ski racing because it all ended badly for me in Dartmouth. I much prefer teaching people how to ski and enjoy the sport outside the confines of ski racing gates. Perhaps I'll do some instructing here in Aspen this winter, I don't know. I wouldn't be opposed to earning some extra coin. Nine hundred bucks a month in rent eats into my wage as a freelancer. Fifty bucks for a story up to three hundred words, seventy five dollars for stories between three hundred and seven fifty, and for the rare beast over a thousand words, I can bill a lofty one hundred dollars.

Up and down the Roaring Fork Valley, from Glenwood Springs to Aspen itself, rent is high. I am living North of Carbondale this winter on a horse farm without internet. Jack helped me find the place. The woman who owns the house leases out the adjacent land on her property to a neighbour well suited for horses. Donna works for the company that owns the four Aspen area ski resorts. Doing what, I don't exactly know. Something in human resources. Her father bequeathed the house to her. She grew up in the thing and then raised a son here who is about my age. No mention of a husband. The son chooses to live in Chicago to work as a software developer. Donna has the upstairs floor and I have the bottom. When I asked her for the mailing address of the property, she didn't know the correct answer. She also never locks the house doors. Even if I wanted to I couldn't because the doors on the old log house are without locks to begin with.

Further up the dirt road several miles past the house, there is a turnout offering jaw dropping views to the south of Mount Sopris (elevation 12,953 ft.). Already on several occasions I have gone up the road to watch the evening light hit the massive peak giving it a soul-warming alpen glow. It's a nice way to end a day. It takes me a good thirty minutes to drive to the Aspen Herald's office in town. I don't mind the commute and have already immensely enjoyed living in the vicinity of horses. While it would be nice to have internet for my job as a journalist, I can make do by frequenting a cafe or going into the Herald's offices of which I am not so much a fan. I do my work better when not around other reporters. I don't know why, I just do. Maybe this will change as I familiarize myself with the paper's staff.

* * *

Right now Aspen is in what locals are calling "off season." This is the time between the busy summer months and ski season which starts this year on Thanksgiving for both Ajax and Highlands. Snowmass and Buttermilk are supposed to open first week of December. These dates of course could change depending on how cold and snowy October and November are.

At Taos, there were mid-November days when at the ski hill, it was snowing like it was the middle of January. But in town, dry, high sixties. I still love skiing Taos and am concerned about the change afoot there as a result of the new owner of the mountain. Billionaire hedge fund manager named Louis Salter. Salter purchased the resort from the founding family and has publicly stated his plans to add an airline, develop the base with brand-name hotels, and install bigger, faster ski lifts. Salter to many locals is robbing the place of its unique identity. But Salter needs to make the ski hill a going concern and I get that.

* * *

I finally met Alyssa last night at a bar that shares the same building as Aspen's ancient Wheeler Opera House. I arrived early, sat at the bar and ordered beer. Sitting next to me was an older man wearing a large cowboy hat and a worn jean jacket. He said his name was Carlos. On his face was a bushy black handlebar moustache greying. Looked like a real salty old rancher. Carlos and I were initiated into conversation by the younger man sitting next to him loud and drunk. His name was Stephen and he'd just got off work as a salesman for an art gallery. He must've been drinking on the job. Stephen wore leather shoes with pointed toes, slacks, and a white collared shirt. His blonde hair, buzzed to the skull. Stephen was talking to Carlos about photography. Carlos saying he used to be an amateur photographer but gave up his hobby with the advent of digital camera technology. He told Stephen and myself that the old way of taking and then developing pictures on film was a lost art. They were talking about photography because this was something the two had in common.

The gallery where Stephen works features photography and nothing but. Carlos was asking about some of the pictures on the wall he had seen as a passerby and Stephen described how the photographer was able to achieve the effect. Stephen took out his phone and showed us photos of pieces newly hung on the wall. An exhibition by a New Zealand photographer popular in New York. I didn't like the photos as they lacked authenticity and looked digital in all the wrong ways. The photo on his phone was of a giant photograph hanging on the gallery's walls, thirty feet long, ten feet tall. A sailboat held in storage with the mast down. Stephen paid his tab and left. Alyssa was running way late leaving Carlos and I alone to chat. At this juncture in his life, he told me his creative outlet was in the radio program he hosted on one of the Roaring Fork's community radio stations. "Down valley radio" as Carlos put it. If the location of anything is anywhere between Glenwood Springs and Aspen but not in Aspen: "down valley." Carlos told me his time slot was an hour each weekday morning. I asked him what he liked to play and he said "alternative stuff." I told Carlos I was a journalist and might do some ski instructing this winter and then he started to tell me about some of the known and lesser so writers of the Aspen area.

One in particular, a woman who wrote historical fiction. She was a best selling author in the sixties. She wrote in the mornings from her Woody Creek cabin and in the afternoons, skied in the winter, fished in the summer. She made plenty of money from her writing and chose to live a quiet life writing and skiing and fishing. Carlos told me he had been living in the area now for forty years, originally from Kansas. He met this author one night in a pub just as I had met him. At that time she was in her seventies. Not long after Carlos met her she died from a heart attack despite being physically fit.

I changed the subject back to his radio show. I wondered if he'd played a few artists I thought alternative. He surprised me by saying yes he knew those artists but no, they were far too mainstream. He said a few unfamiliar names and said that I could always listen to his show even if I wasn't able to on the appointed hour. Each show of his was on the radio station's website.

Alyssa finally arrived and when she did, Carlos took it as a queue to leave.

"Who was that?" Alyssa asked sitting down.

"Dunno. Stranger I just met. Guy has a radio show in town."

"Hi by the way, I'm Alyssa. Sorry I'm late."

"Meko. No problem."

Alyssa ordered tequila, I stuck with beer. We made our introductions, sharing cherry picked pieces of our own histories. Alyssa said she was new to Aspen taking a year off from college to live with her dad. She grew up in Atlanta, and as soon as she left home for college in Athens, her parents divorced. Dad got a new job and life in Aspen. Mom remarried and stayed in Atlanta. Alyssa said she wanted to build her portfolio as a photographer and get away from Athens for a while.

"Why? I asked.

"Need a break. When dad moved here, I thought what a perfect time to finally get out of Georgia."

"You studying photography?"

"Ha! No. What's there to study? I'm self taught. No, my major's marketing."

"I've heard you're a pretty good photographer."

"Yeah? Who said that?"

"Norman."

"Awe. He's so cute." I laughed.

"Heard you're not a bad writer yourself."

"Thanks."

"When you make deadline..."

"That didn't take long."

"Word gets around."

"Yeah, fast."

"Aspen's a small town."

We went on like this for a few more drinks. Didn't take long for Alyssa to loosen up. Before long, she was cracking jokes with anyone who'd listen. She was genuinely a funny person. Kind of crazy, but just the right amount. That was my first impression of Alyssa. A good one. I left the bar beer buzzed with the impression there were characters in this town. I had grunt work to do the following day on the story involving the Korean break-in. I had a scheduled call in the morning with Chung's lawyer about the legal process transferring Chung from his Pitkin County jail cell back to Seoul. Yesterday, Norman said good luck to me on the phone after giving me the contact information for Chung's lawyer. It had not been easy for Norman, or so he told me, to get access to the "white shoe" representing Chung whose firm does work for the Korean government. His name is Ari Cohen.

* * *

While waiting to make the call, I listened to Carlos' show, liking what I heard. All of it was new to me, and here I was thinking I had a good handle on music. Ari and I spoke for two minutes. All he said to me was that he was flying to Aspen next week, we could talk more then. As soon as I got off the phone with him I told Norman who then said to save the story for yet another week. Fine by me, however I could use the cash. I told Norman as much, prompting his assignment to me of a two hundred fifty word story due at the end of the day about the Aspen Valley Ski Club. At five I hit the send button on an email to Norman with the story attached. As soon as I received the assignment, I called the club's alpine director who gave me the scoop on when they were hoping to start their season. Quick work, easy money. Made the deadline.

* * *

I have a date tonight with a girl that I swiped right to on a dating app. She's from Aspen and works at the Pitkin County Library. First we are going for a short hike up Smuggler Mountain on the north edge of Aspen. Dinner and drinks afterward. I have three hundred bucks to my name right now which makes me wonder if I should be taking girls out. Life has its priorities though and woman are at the top. I was grateful when, earlier this week, Norman said if I needed some more work, a buddy of his owns an irrigation company. I told Norman that would be helpful and he gave me the contact of his friend.

* * *

I took Eve, thirty-two, strawberry blonde, to an Aspen steakhouse after our walk. We sat at the bar for its menu, considerably cheaper than the dining room's. Twenty bucks for a steak sandwich and too many fries. Eve and I were impressed by the bordello inspired interior design of the restaurant sitting no more than fifty. Taxidermy, antique photos of Aspen skiing, that kind of thing. It was a busy night in the little restaurant and we were treated well by the Argentinean bartender who also served our food.

We split the cheapest red and I am still embarrassed at my question to the bartender as to whether the bottle could be corked. Eve and the bartender teased me because they just assumed we would drink the bottle in its entirety before exiting into the cool October night. In a show, I threw up my hands as if to give in to the notion that I would be leaving drunk. I smiled at Eve, our eyes met. She took her gaze downward to the restaurant floor. I could tell that she was nervous at meeting me in person. Perhaps to her, the prospect of wine was nothing more than tonic for her nerves. I found her to be attractive but not quite as attractive as what the photos on the dating app implied. Maybe she was thinking the same of me.

Equal parts embarrassment and ambivalence course through me on my decision to use dating apps to meet women. I figure though that since I am new to this town, how else can I so quickly arrange to meet available women.

Eve was born and raised here which, when she told me, I couldn't help but express surprise. She said it was true that she was a minority when compared to the many who make the move here to live a life at the base of four ski areas. Most of her friends growing up moved away to America's urban centres, places like Los Angeles, New York and of course Denver. I don't know if it is right to assume, but I can't help but think that if you grew up in Aspen, your parents must have a few bucks in the bank. If for no other reason than by reverse mortgaging a house purchased twenty, thirty years ago to take advantage of the town's runaway real estate prices.

Eve said she studied communications and journalism at the University of Utah. She was thrilled to meet someone actually working as a journalist. I of course did not study journalism and think to do so a waste of time, money and energy. Is journalism nothing more than asking questions? I kept these thoughts to myself. I asked her what she did for work in Aspen. She said she works as a ski instructor in the winter months and in the other months, part time at the library.

Naturally a discussion of ski instruction followed and I told her of my background in skiing. She was impressed at my racing history and asked why I was no longer involved in the sport. I said that if she still is interested in knowing the answer, I would tell her another time. There were more interesting topics to cover on date numero uno. I made sure to ask her whether she could ever use some help instructing or knew of how to get a foot in the door teaching on Ajax. She liked that I knew of and referred to the ski area as Ajax. Ajax is a much better name than Aspen Mountain and Eve and I toasted on that just as our calamari arrived. I looked at the dish, impressive as it was, and the alcohol around us, and I took a deep breath at the thought of what the bill would be. I wasn't going to let Eve pay, no way in hell. Even if she asked which I hoped she would.

Over fried squid we talked more about Ajax and the culture she was distinctly privy to as a local and instructor. Like referring to the mountain's lifts not by their trail map names but by number. Ajax Express is lift 3, Shadow Mountain: 1A, FIS: 6, Bell: 5, Ruthie's is 8 and so on. She told me about the Shrines, Ski Gangs, Dumps, Trainor's Ridge, Blake Mamba, and the route of the old world cup downhill through Aztec. She knew it all. One of her clients, she said, has two young daughters who like to ski fast. She asked if maybe I would be willing to teach them some racing techniques. The Coutinho's would be flying up from Rio de Janeiro for the holidays for three to four weeks. I thanked her and said I would be happy to if in a couple months those plans remained in place. With some wine in us, we became more at ease and we looked at each other for a while without saying much.

* * *

I am wide awake writing this journal at twenty past three in the morning and no, Eve isn't sleeping in my bed. I don't normally eat and drink as much as I did tonight and now my stomach is punishing me as it negotiates the rich steak sandwich, wine, fries and calamari. We spent over two hours in the steakhouse and the bill came to one hundred and eighteen dollars with tip. So now I have less than two hundred bucks to my name and I can't help but think my anxiety over such a matter is also contributing to this sleepless night. On one hand I enjoy the notion of being close to broke because there is a freedom in such a situation. That enlightened attitude toward personal finance does not always come easy.

The thought of my limited resources prompted me to send a text, despite the hour, to Norman's irrigation friend, Pete Christopher. That was the first thing I did when I woke with a start fifteen minutes ago. I really hope he will need me for help. I want to see more of Eve. Maybe Alyssa, too. Norman said Pete leaves Aspen at the end of every October to follow the water fowls from the Dakotas down to the Gulf as a bird hunting guide. There is roughly two weeks remaining until he takes off.

Eve and I left the restaurant together and since she lives in town she walked home to her apartment she shares with two others. I took the bus down to Carbondale and then hitched a ride with someone driving in a direction toward the horse farm. I was too drunk to drive home and left my vehicle parked in front of the steakhouse. I was lucky to find a ride to my place given that it was pitch black, almost midnight, and the only sounds I could hear stepping off the bus were the yips of coyotes not all that far off. The woman who picked me up lived further past my place. She knew who I was already since Donna and her of course know each other well enough for my arrival to have come up in their conversation.

Eve gave me a peck on the cheek after I walked her to her apartment on the west end of Aspen. I blushed deeply. She said before I closed the door to call her. I said I would.

* * *

Today was a challenge. I can't sleep-in, so I felt utterly hollow after my sleepless night when I got up at my usual six bells. My only hope was that by writing this down I would feel I did something of value. When I remembered around noontime after six cups of coffee that my truck was parked outside the steakhouse, it took all my physical and mental energy to make the journey up valley for its retrieval. On the bus ride to town, it was a nice surprise to find the Maroon Creek bridge not being worked on as it had through the previous week. The time required to travel over the bridge while the workers worked was akin to an LA rush hour. There is one road into and out of Aspen and the traffic can stack quickly. When I saw the parking ticket lodged between the windshield and its wipers, I cursed loudly. The amount, thirty five bucks, is trivial but not when expressed as a sizeable percentage of my current net worth.

Standing beside my truck, parking ticket in hand, I looked at it with as much insight possible given my sleep deprived level of cognition. I have Land of Enchantment plates on my truck, how will the town of Aspen enforce this fee upon me? My hunch is that parking tickets can go unpaid so long as I don't keep getting them. I crumpled up the ticket and threw it over my shoulder, climbed in and turned the ignition. I cursed even louder when I saw a light in my dash indicating low fuel levels. Why hadn't I filled up last night to avoid this situation? I was now faced with a choice. Would I have enough in the tank to get me to the Conoco at the Aspen Business Centre several miles out of town? Or should I hedge my bets and go to the gas station in town where prices are considerably higher? To hell with it, what else is on my schedule today, was my thinking. If I ran out of gas between town and the ABC, then at least I will know the limitations of my dear old truck.

Well, let me tell you, I was happy to make it to the ABC. The thing started sputtering as I turned off the highway into the station. My relief was tempered when I saw all the pumps being used with queues behind them. I was in no shape to idle my starved vehicle and so committed a faux pas by scooting past a Prius ahead of me in a queue to a newly free pump. The granola bar driving the Prius squawked at me when he eventually arrived to his own pump. I ignored it and looked to the west as I filled. I put fifteen bucks in and left without again looking in the direction of the Prius.

Before leaving town to Carbondale, I made sure to pick up a Herald. I was keen to see if my name was spelt correctly. My pleasure in seeing 'Torres' was curbed after I read my short little story. Whoever copy edited it made spelling mistakes that weren't my own. I couldn't believe what I was reading. My little story about the ski club appeared as if someone else entirely had written it. With spelling mistakes. But I had no energy in me to let this anger and embarrassment run through the rest of my day. It is baffling when I think about it. How someone could change a writer's work to lesser quality and think that it was better. Without even asking. It makes me already unwilling to continue writing for this outfit. When the time comes and I publish something of weight, how will I have any sort of confidence in how it's published? Like I said, today was a challenge.

The bright note was a favourable reply from Pete Christopher who called me later in the afternoon. Pete said that yes, he could certainly use my help come Monday morning. I couldn't tell if the voice I was hearing on the other line was coming from a man already a few beers deep or whether that was just the way he spoke. In any event, he took it upon himself to ask all sorts of questions about who I was, why I was in Aspen and so on. I did the same to him and from what I gathered, here was a middle aged guy who was born and raised in Aspen, knows everyone, who used to ski but can't anymore on account of bad knees. He has five dogs (two labs, three German short-hairs). All are expertly trained pointers for hunting bird. They travel with him wherever he goes including on the job. "We got two weeks before I am outta here and three hundred houses to clear the lines before winter." He told me to meet him at the Brush Creek intercept lot Monday morning, seven bells. Having good honest work lined up, I was soon out like a light.

* * *

I am three days into my tenure as an irrigation man, and I am exhausted. Taking the time to write this journal is a Herculean effort made only easier knowing there's two days remaining before the weekend. Not that I will have time off. I'll be busy writing stories for the Herald. Ari Cohen arrived today and earlier this evening we met for the big interview. We went for cocktails and he picked up the bill. I have three Old Fashioneds in me and perhaps this is what is fuelling tonight's missive.

Ari came across initially as guarded and lawyerly and slick. Altogether, boring. Thankfully he was thirsty and his five cocktails loosened him up nicely to a more frank discussion of what was going on with his client. He noticed my dirty irrigation hands after his second cocktail and asked if I was on the agriculture beat for the paper. I declared with pride my honest work of clearing irrigation lines and the lawyer at first looked at me like I was a bit off but then came around to understand where I was coming from, I think anyway.

The previous three days of irrigation were eventful. On Monday, I met Pete at the intercept lot where he gave me a run down on the day. I was to work with him on day one, the rest of the week I would join a different crew. I left my truck at the lot and asked if I needed to pay for parking. The answer, a blessed no. Into Pete's van I climbed and his five beloved dogs greeted me with gusto. The older of the two labs looked at me scornfully for I, a stranger, was taking her seat. Kate reluctantly went to the back of the vehicle where the four others energetically sniffed, wagged, and wrestled as dogs do. I asked Pete about his dogs and he spoke of them with sublime adoration. Kate was the oldest by a few years and the other lab, Babe was the youngest. The three German short-hairs all were of similar age and their names: Oscar, Fleming, Faulkner. Pete had a strange look and way about him but I had a feeling his heart was whole.

He was chewing cannabis infused gummy's by noon and those did wonders to open up communication channels. It was a cold, silent morning before the gummy's came into the picture. The dogs, Pete and I went to work and at first it was certainly an adjustment for me to get the hang of it. My back wasn't used to the motions required to complete the job at hand. And the homes we visited, good lord. I am not one to gawk at the homes of others but I couldn't help it traipsing around the well manicured lawns of these properties worth no less than eight figures.

After lunch quickly enjoyed while driving to our next job, I asked Pete if he knew where Carlyle Erikson lived. By this time, his crusty, monosyllabic exterior was gone. At my mention of Erikson's name, he let out a sort of horse laugh. He asked if I'd heard of the story about the "Asian dude." I said I was quite familiar with it given that I was reporting the story for a future Herald piece. Pete asked what I knew. After I was done telling him, he laughed even louder, eventually asking Kate if he should tell me what really happened. Kate, now at ease enough with my presence to sit on my lap, looked at Pete without emotion and turned to look out the window at the palatial Red Mountain houses passing by. A bear of a Golden Retriever waltzed across the front lawn of a compound. I wondered, did Kate want to know what kind of dog could afford to live in such a place?

Pete took Kate's silence as reason to not tell me what he knew. I pleaded. As I did, he looked at me with intense suspicion. He said, "what makes you think I can trust you?" I apologized for my imposition and a then long awkward silence followed. Made more awkward by Pete turning the radio off. Finally Pete erupted with laughter saying he was only kidding and why was I white in the face? The story he told was nothing short of strange. Pete isn't the most articulate. He started telling one story, which intersected with another, that was tangentially connected to a third. He couldn't finish a sentence and would start a new one with a relative clause. "Whereas, I don't think it's a big deal..." and so on. But, he did mention The Syndicate. What's the Syndicate, I asked. His answer was short and loopy. What I gathered, was that it was a group of people in the Aspen area quietly making big bucks selling contraband goods and somehow Chung was connected. I wanted to know more. But that was all I was getting today.

When the time came for me to have cocktails with Ari, I was unsure whether to hold my cards close to my chest on what Pete told me or let it all out on what "word on the street" was concerning the Chung break-in. Pete is a good irrigation man and friend of the dog; yet still I am unsure of how much I can trust him. I called Norman on my way to see Ari asking his advice. All he said to me was that I need be careful of what that "slippery fox" claims as fact.

Both drinks and conversation with Ari Cohen started stiff. The latter progressively less so compared to the former. He told me he wasn't in town for long and this was his first time west of the Mississippi. He asked about what it was like reporting on avalanches. He wasn't concealing his Manhattan snobbery. He told me of the several art galleries he was hoping to visit before flying back to New York. I caught him off guard when I told him which of the ones he was planning to visit were still open despite off season.

He asked: "You know art?"

"A bit, yeah. It's in the family, have a degree in art history."

"Oh? From where?"

I told him about Dartmouth, Taos and my mother's gallery. He became animated. He slurped down what remained of his second cocktail and yelled from across the room to the bartender for more. He apologized for his being prim toward me. "I just assumed everyone here only skis and smokes dope," he said. To which I said that is probably true but those two interests didn't necessarily preclude other interests.

All the while I was talking to Cohen, in the back of my mind I was having a furious debate over whether I should bring up what Pete had told me about Chung and the Syndicate. I was nervous, and when I think about it as I write this, I am not entirely sure why. Perhaps the way the conversation unfolded gives my hindsight unfair bias. It was when the lawyer started cracking politically incorrect jokes that I thought, to hell with it. He was clearly not as square as most of the lawyers I'd dealt with as a journalist. After he finished telling me a joke about a woman's very large "opening," as he put it, I brought up the subject of why we were meeting in the first place: Won Seok Chung. Right as I said his client's name, Cohen said, "fuck, fine. Here we go," and ordered another round. This was to be my last but he would need another few before our rendezvous came to a close.

I asked, "Is it true?"

Cohen: "Is what true?"

"Why don't you start with telling me your version of the story."

"I thought you knew by now, Chung thought he was breaking into the house of that Erikson guy claiming mental instability."

"Well of course I know that side of the story, but I am talking about another side of the story." Cohen nervously looked around the room.

I said, "this isn't a case you wish to be involved with, now is it?"

"Not the least bit. Truth is, I am doing this as a favour for some people that helped me out in the past...which is neither here nor there."

"Fair enough, so you would agree there is more to this story."

"I'm surprised it took you, what, a whole week to figure that out? What have you heard? By the way this is off the record and if the contents of this conversation end up on the public record, remember, I'm a lawyer."

"You need not be concerned."

"So what have you heard?"

"I won't say unless I can be sure you will tell me whether it's accurate or not."

"Deal."

"Well, what I've heard is the foll—" Just as I was about to reveal what Pete had told me, someone from behind shouted my name. I turned to see that it was my Guatemalan irrigation crew-mate of the past two days. He was inviting me over for a drink.

Cohen: "Who's that?"

"Alfredo. Colleague."

"At the paper?"

"No, in irrigation."

"Well, go on then, go say hello...and bring me back another drink will you?"

Alfredo was there to have a drink at the bar with his girlfriend who worked as a bartender. She was a petite latino with a tight ponytail and attractive features. Alfredo had done well. We had a brief conversation for his English was good but not great. I told him I was in a meeting for my other job and when I ordered the drink for Cohen, Alfredo said that it was on the house thinking it was for me. I objected but his girl-friend refused my cash. I thanked them both and returned to Cohen busy scrolling through his phone. He asked why only the one drink and I told him I had had my fill to which he shrugged.

He said, "Well, go on then, what do you know?"

"Apparently the break-in was no accident."

Cohen smiling: "That right?"

"Apparently, Chung and Erikson happen to know each other, quite well in fact."

Cohen, still smiling: "How well?"

When I told him the rest of what I knew, about the elusive Syndicate, Cohen had only one thing to say: "Who the hell is your source?"

"Some bird hunter," I said. Cohen, now drunk, howled. I wanted to know more about the Syndicate but on that subject, Cohen was a closed book.

He picked up the tab and invited me to join him the next day on a visit to Chung. I said I would and we parted. Alfredo, still at the bar, saw me make an exit and yelled to me something in Spanish. Alfredo and I get along great on the job and enjoy talking about the various meals we enjoy cooking for the women in our lives. Yesterday he gave me tips on improving my turkey mole recipe while I told him about how best to fillet wild caught trout.

The next day I was picked up at the intercept lot just after eight by Alfredo. He was driving one of Pete's company vans. When the vehicle pulled in, I stepped out from my truck and the man sitting next to Alfredo did the same. His name, Yasiel. Yasiel gave me shotgun and sat in the back. Alfredo said that Yasiel would prefer to sit in the back and that his English was poor. He was hired, like me, for the end of season rush. When we got to the first house to do our work, Alfredo was kind, efficient and expedient in setting the tone for how the tasks would be split among the three of us. Between rapid fire Spanish directed toward Yasiel and broken English for me, we found ourselves a nice work rhythm clearing out irrigation lines. As the morning and day unfolded, I slowly learned more about my colleagues.

Alfredo came to Aspen thirteen years ago and has worked for Pete every spring, summer and fall. In the winter months, Alfredo works for a company setting up holiday decorations. His signature phrase was to kindly say "si mon" whenever 'yes' was the required answer. Alfredo lives in Old Snowmass in a porta-trailer type unit with his girlfriend. Cheap rent and walking distance down a hill to a fishable river. They rarely see each other which Alfredo said, laughing, was for the better on account of their relentless work schedules. Alfredo works three-hundred sixty days a year and Pete later told me that he owns a couple houses in rural Guatemala he rarely visits due to immigration hassle. He said he used to work at a mid-mountain restaurant on Highlands that's the number two distributor of a fancy Champagne sold around the world. Alfredo said he used to get drunk and do a tonne of coke almost every day while working as a line cook. 'Coh-kah-een' was his pronunciation. Now, at age thirty-five, he lives to work, rarely drinks and won't even look at the white powder. We started talking about books, and he told me he likes to pass the time by reading the New Testament.

Sensing my inquisitive nature, Alfredo took it upon himself to tell me a bit about Yasiel. The language barrier proved too formidable when I tried doing so directly with the man himself. Alfredo said Yasiel came to Aspen from the Sinaloa province of Mexico and is four years Alfredo's senior despite looking twenty. He's been in Aspen for twelve years and was introduced to Alfredo by Yasiel's uncle. He is a quiet, industrious worker and is kind in suggesting by demonstration more efficient ways to do my job. I only heard him raise his voice once in the time we worked together. We came across a black bear one morning rummaging through trash cans in a client's backyard. "Correr!" he said. "Correr!" Yasiel has two sons: the eldest, twenty and the second, three. His new wife is in her early twenties and Yasiel does all of the cooking and housework. He has a soft, high pitched voice and everything about him makes him seem the least likely candidate to be a former employee of one of the most dangerous Mexican drug cartels. Which Alfredo said comes with the cartel trade. Anyone in the Roaring Fork Valley with any trace of involvement with the Sinaloa cartel, past or present, are masters at leaving no trace. Ghost-like. Alfredo said Yasiel is an impressive, self taught cook and I don't doubt it when I look at what his lunches consist of as compared to my pathetic ham sandwiches. Chorizo tamales, homemade corn tortillas, that kind of thing.

Work with my irrigation comrades was honest and direct. We worked and said little and completed our tasks as required. The high country sun beat down upon us and we each shed layers of clothing as the mornings wore on. Not once did we encounter the inhabitants of the houses we did our work on. Lights off, locked shut. As distant and remote to us as locked up Buddhist monasteries in the eastern Himalaya. Where are these people? What do they do? Alfredo occasionally told me what little he knew. How the owner of one particular compound was an international arms dealer. To which I could only nod in wonderment. We didn't say much about it, preferring to work on the houses while Canadian geese honked overhead on their flight south. Here and there I would look up from the task at hand to see far off in the distance ski trails on a mountainside belonging to either of Ajax, Buttermilk or Highlands. It wouldn't be long before I would find myself on those very trails.

My mother likes to say skiing is the closest thing to parachuting out of an airplane. She is quoting my deceased father who told her of the similar sensations after his bootcamp training and before leaving to Northern Kuwait and never returning. He too grew up skiing Taos Valley. My mother said she was always happier on a pair of cross-country skis after my dad's death. Alfredo said he likes to ski but can only ever get in a couple days per season. I suggested one day we try and go. "Si mon," he said turning his gaze toward the mountains. The tone in his voice suggested to me the likelihood of us lining up our schedules was low. We returned to our work without another word spoken. The silence was wonderful. Eventually broken by him asking me about what the women were like in Taos. Talk of women, perfect subject matter for the hard physical labour before us.

* * *

Last week I sent Norman a publishable version of the Chung imbroglio. Of course, it helped immensely to have Chung speak more frankly to me under the guidance of his lawyer. Ari sat the whole time next to his client as Chung and I conversed. I felt bad for having to knock off early from my irrigation work to be on time for the meeting I had with Chung and Cohen. I was leaving Alfredo and Yasiel with more work to do than they anticipated that day. When Alfredo picked me up at the intercept lot that Thursday morning we didn't say much, as per usual for the past three days, but I told him that because of my other job, I only would be able to help until noon. "Si, mon." We were listening to loud 80's music on the radio. Alfredo would always turn up the 80's when not listening to traditional Mexican. The latter of which I know he prefers. The 80's music, played to appease the gringo sitting next to him.

That morning, Alfredo told me Pete had a pay check ready for me since it was that time of the month. Although I had only worked three and half days, I was grateful to know that soon my bank account would show a few hundred. I didn't even know what my hourly wage was. I was just happy for the work. It kept me busy. And I would also be receiving my first pay check from the Herald. Whatever would I do with my newfound riches? I was thinking of Eve. That is, if she will still talk to me after my clumsy radio silence. Perhaps I'll take her to the Wheeler for a ski movie everyone is talking about debuting this weekend. I have never been one to enjoy ski movies. Skiing is to be done, not watched. But I figure Eve to be the type to salivate over new releases every fall. Most people who ski like ski movies. I'm just not one of those people. Seeing the inside of the ancient Wheeler would be enough reason for me to go. And now that I have the Chung story out of the way (for now anyway), I feel a weight has lifted from my shoulders.

Am I happy with how it turned out? Well, to see the eight-hundred fifty word feature on page two of the Monday paper, that was a nice feeling. Was there spelling errors in the story that were of someone else's doing? Yes. At least the copy editor didn't change the structure of my piece too egregiously. And my name was spelled right! I asked Norman about this issue in the most polite way I could think possible and before he could give me an answer, his phone rang. I sat there while he talked for a good ten minutes. When he ended the call he said he had another assignment for me if I wanted. Part of me thinks it's Norman making the mistakes rather than this elusive copy editor. I haven't yet seen someone in the office I haven't met and no one has told me their job is that of copy editing. I will give him benefit of the doubt that if the mistakes are his, they are being made as a byproduct of him being overworked and underpaid.

The new story is about subject matter I have no experience with. Kim Chandler has written the social scene column in the paper for close to twenty years. For the paper's weekend issue, there is a magazine supplement that has two pages of Kim's photographs and a few words about Aspen's social-sphere. The event that I am to go to this Saturday night, the night before the ski movie premiere, is a fundraising silent auction dinner for the Westcott Foundation, a local non-profit organization involved with Native American economic development. I am to dress up and take photos of groups of people and be sure to get their names. I asked Alyssa to join me but she was already booked. Kim went into labor with her second child and it was her husband on the phone with Norman to inform him she would be on maternity leave.

Norman said he wanted me to fill her shoes for the upcoming event, and if things turned out well, perhaps the column would be mine until Kim's return. I accepted the assignment. In my journalism, I am above no story. The prospect of at least one story per week bodes well for me. Irrigation work will only last for another week and ski season is still a good three to four away. Norman assured me that if I did get the column, I wouldn't be shut out of any opportunities to report on front page news material. The response the paper got from the Chung story was receptive. I personally thought there would be more shock and awe from the community. I told as much to Pete who reminded me, after he asked if the Meko Torres he read in the paper was really me, that the "shit that goes on in this town" means that there is always at least one Hollywood B-movie story per week. On the next page after the Chung story (that had no mention of the Syndicate - Norman said we needed more evidence), there was a story about a local real estate broker charged for holding three people at gunpoint on Independence Pass.

* * *

I received a phone call from Alfredo before the fundraiser. He asked if I needed more work helping Yasiel's uncle rake leaves before the first snow. Without hesitation, I said yes. Snow fell heavy from the night sky as I walked from my truck over to the St. Regis. I entered the hotel with snowy hair and speculation that my new raking job of only a few minutes ago was in jeopardy. Remembering that I was at the hotel with a job to do for pay helped me forget my raking blues. I was dressed for the evening in a suit I found at a thrift shop earlier. Fourteen bucks for a shirt, tie, slacks and blazer. For shoes, I borrowed a pair of Yasiel's gleaming black snake skin loafers. He got them from a friend's uncle in Ciudad Juarez before crossing to Texas.

I looked in a mirror before I left my house and thought I looked pretty sharp. I combed my hair back and shaved. I was thinking surely there'd be some girls there for me to flirt with. That indeed was the case. I took lots of photos and got lots of names and numbers and drank wine and felt like I was the most charming guy in the building. "Where's Kim? Oh well, we like you" - I was getting a lot of that. I met a girl from Starkville, Mississippi and she had the thickest southern accent I'd ever heard. Her name, Lyons, and she wasn't shy about asking me right off the bat if I was Indian. I said I was part Tiwa Indian, Mexican, Spanish. Lyons was of German heritage and nothing but. She said I had a different look and that she likes different. "That's all you're getting with me," I lamely replied. She laughed, rolled her eyes and grabbed me by the arm for a drink. I followed her to a wine bar draped with white linen. She ordered a white, red for myself. I told her what I was up to and she asked if she could help.

"In what way," I asked.

"Tellin' you who you're takin' pictures of."

"I don't mind asking them."

"Save your breath, I'll just tell you."

"Oh you know a few of these people?"

"Know 'em all."

I wasn't sure how someone could know the names of all the several hundred guests in attendance. I asked her how she managed. She said she worked for the company that produced the event and was in charge of putting together the guest list. I apologized.

"I was curious who Kim's replacement would be when we heard she wouldn't be able to make it."

"I know she's missed...doin' my best."

"Let me introduce you to some friends of mine," she said as she again grabbed me by the arm leading me over to an older couple. "This is Ted and May Gaffney, they should be in your column."

I took their photo and introduced myself. I felt a bit strange to take their photo and then try and talk to them like it never happened. Lyons began talking to May which freed up Ted to speak directly with me.

Ted asked, "You the same Torres that wrote that story about the Korean?" I said I was and he told me he knew Cohen.

"I was around when Cohen's bosses used to defend the drug dealers who got busted here in the 80's."

"Didn't know that."

"Cohen didn't tell you about his firm's history here?"

"No he kept that one to himself."

"Probably assumed you knew."

"Most people do?"

"Locals, anyway."

The story Pete told me about Chung, the one that never made it to print, all of a sudden had a great deal more plausibility. Pete had said a few days after first mentioning the Syndicate that Chung was connected to an illegal cigarette distribution business overseen by Native Americans with connections to the Sinaloa cartel that had people like Sheriff Bledsoe in their pocket. The Carlyle Erikson part of the story was meant to act as a smoke screen against what really happened. Chung did in fact break into a house but the real target of his wasn't Erikson (although Erikson supposedly too is affiliated with the business). It was a high ranking member of the gang that distributed the illicit tobacco Chung was in charge of moving across the water. There had been a disagreement and that was the extent of Pete's story. I asked Ted about the rumoured disagreement and Ted shot me a glance before asking what I had heard.

"That's all I've heard, that there was a disagreement." Ted looked at me.

He said, "I've heard a few things."

"Perhaps those things could be discussed in more detail in a different setting."

"You really want to know?"

"Yes."

Before I could get a word in another word, Lyons was pulling me in a new direction. "They're from Texas, been coming to Aspen forever," she said.

Lyons knew them through her uncle who lives in Aspen and works as a contributing editor for a big New York magazine.

"Ted and I are going for beers sometime."

"Doesn't take long for you to make friends," she said.

"This is more for work."

"Ted having a party soon?"

"That's not all I write about."

"No? What else?"

"Wrote a story published this week about a Korean criminal trespasser."

"Oh, I saw that one. That was you?"

"Yes it was."

"I thought it was good...a few spelling mistakes."

"Don't remind me."

"Well I hope Ted can help you out."

Lyons gave me her number and we parted ways for the rest of the evening. I met more people than I can remember. It was midnight when I finally got back to my place. Before calling it a night, I sent a message to Lyons. She replied almost immediately and now I am having dialogue with three girls of interest. I'm in a good spot.

* * *

This morning I banged away for a couple hours typing up the column. I was only given one hundred words to work with since the photos take up most of the spread. One hundred words to describe the party was easy. And since the weekend supplement had different advertisers than the weekly paper, I was paid seventy-five bucks rather than thirty had it been published in the Herald. Norman sent me an email after lunch telling me he thought I did a good job and said it was my column until I left or Kim returned. I accepted the offer and was excited at what next week's event would be.

I sent Lyons a message first thing in the morning. "Hi. You're amazing." I also sent a message to Eve asking her if she was still keen to go to the movie premiere at the Wheeler. She replied yes, that she would buy the tickets for us online. Twenty minutes later I got a message from her saying she happened to purchase the last ticket available before the event sold out. She had one, but not one for me. I told her not to worry, that I would still try and go. Maybe there'd be scalpers.

* * *

Once again, I'm wide awake writing this down after a night out with Eve. When I picked her up at her apartment before the show, she suggested I park my truck at her place and we walk the short distance to the opera house. It was a cold night and on the way into town, we came across a big black bear in an alleyway rummaging for food. Eve took a photo of the bear and posted it to her Instagram account laughing. She wanted my help coming up with a clever caption to go along with the photo of the bear. I said I wasn't good at that stuff and let her come up with something on her own. She said, "But aren't you a writer?" A lightbulb went off and she rapidly tapped something into her phone, giggled to herself, and then put her phone away. I didn't bother asking, nor did I care what she came up with. When I told her, after she asked, that I wasn't on any social media, she looked at me in awe. "How can you live like that?" she said. I shrugged my shoulders and led her by the hand through the Wheeler's front doors. She had her ticket's barcode on her phone and after having it scanned by the doorman, went to grab two seats before all were taken.

I started asking people in the busy lobby if anyone had an extra ticket. After a few minutes being denied, I was feeling like tonight wasn't my night. The show was about to start and everyone was filing in through the doors, past the doorman, up the stairs to their seats. I overheard a man offer an extra ticket to a friend as they walked by. I asked the guy if he had another. To my surprise and good fortune he did. I asked him how much but he just gave it to me. I thanked him many times, got by the doorman and bolted up the stairs. My head was down as I jumped up every other step. I almost collided with someone walking down. It was Eve. She was coming to see if I had had any luck. I apologized for almost steamrolling her. Up we went to the seats she had saved for us. To my horror, I saw Lyons sitting in the same aisle.

Eve had us seated centre left in the middle of the auditorium. Lyons was on the far right side. I thanked my lucky stars that we entered the room's left side. I definitely saw Lyons and maybe she saw me. I don't know. Throughout the movie, I had trouble thinking of anything else except if Lyons saw me sitting with Eve. I'd been told by Alfredo and Alyssa that Aspen is a small place. Tonight was the first time Aspen felt small. What were the chances we three would be sitting in the same aisle? I didn't even think to look over to see who Lyons was sitting with. Could be another guy, who knows. After the film was over, I darted out of the auditorium before the lights came up telling Eve I had to go to the restroom. While that was true, my escape had everything to do with avoiding seeing Lyons on our way out. I told Eve I would be waiting outside for her.

Like the last time I wrote about a night out with this woman, I am wide awake in the wee hours writing this and no, she isn't in the same bedroom. We walked back to her apartment, and I got in my truck to go down valley. At least tonight I got a peck on the lips which was wonderful. I told her she could come back with me, but she said no she was going to ski A-Basin tomorrow with friends and needed to get up at six. A-Basin had opened its earliest in twenty years. Skiing in October on a resort: Eve was so into the sport, she wouldn't mind major crowds elbowing their way down one measly run open to the public. She said I could come if I want but I declined saying that kind of skiing just wasn't for me. She understood and I said goodnight. I got in my truck and felt great. On KDNK was happy Tom Waits; I turned it loud.

* * *

On 60 Minutes last night, there was a story about the Moai statues of Easter Island. The story was about the conflict the island was experiencing juggling sustainability and mass tourism. One of the local Easter Islanders said on camera that for the contemporary locals, there never had been a time with such material wealth. In material terms, the island was doing better than ever. Overcrowding from tourists however was the price paid for the island's material gain. The story told was really about what a society is willing to sacrifice. Is Easter Island a microcosm perhaps for how we as a people are treating the natural world? I can't help but try and draw parallels between Easter Island and a place like Aspen.

In Aspen, we have a town in the middle of the United States home to some of the planet's wealthiest people. Goods and services sold in town: clothes, homes, furniture, food, can be found at prices higher than the gross incomes of entire cities and towns found around the world. In Aspen, material wealth and success are everywhere one looks. Is this sustainable? The ancient building materials used to construct the Moai statues erode with time. The slow pace of which means we are only now starting to see startling examples of the statues in ruin. On Easter Island, the very feature of a place that is driving such an economic boom is in fact in decline.

More money is invested every year in making ski conditions better, better, better. More snow, more people, more money; rinse, repeat. Growth in the bottom line and a better user experience. Win-win. I don't know how a place like Aspen will look in one hundred years.

Part of me never wants to know, but I can't help but wonder. A local Aspen legend turned one hundred years old the other day. He was interviewed for the Herald by another reporter who quoted him saying there was never a better time than now in Aspen's history. And tomorrow would be better. Could all this fuss over planning the future, developing, sustainability, be nothing more than a state of mind? We can choose a positive or negative outlook on anything. It's our choice. Maybe Aspen will only continue to improve. Maybe Easter Island is in the best material position ever and maybe the success isn't mutually exclusive to the island's environmental sustainability. Perhaps the man interviewed simply needs to change his perspective, his choice alone. His neighbour for all we know may have this exact opinion but was not chosen to be interviewed on camera. Does 60 Minutes create stories or report them? Of course there is institutional bias to contend with on what stories end up being told. As one of my art history professors said, fact is nothing more than a winning argument.

* * *

Today I'm on the horse farm and I won't be going anywhere else. I want to visit the horses, observe them, be around them. Toby, the largest of the six quarter horses in the field was testy with me when I first moved here. I tried to ride him but he wouldn't have any of it. I gave up after a few days and then an iron curtain fell between us. The other day, I patted him while feeding oats to another of the horses. I think it may be his sister, June. His tail fluttered nervously and he made a sort of huff one doesn't associate with horse. I got the message but wasn't about to shower my love over him. Ours was a relationship forged on minimal. Our outlooks were now both aligning positive, but why push it any further than a simple pat on the back.

Reflecting on where I was, what I'd given thought to, could I maybe pitch a backwoodsy style column about the parallels to be found between the backyards of Aspen and the mainstream stories told about the world? I felt confident after nailing the previous social column and having a page two story my first month in town. Norman may just be in the mood to hear some new pitches for the ancient paper going strong since 1895. I looked over to the adjoining property and saw an older man walking from his farm house's front porch with a shotgun in his right hand. I walked over to introduce myself and of course ask about the gun. He said there was a mountain lion in the area "paying a visit tonight." I asked how he figured, to which he said he'd been watching its movement the past several days.

I hadn't the slightest clue there was a mountain lion in the area which just goes to show how inept I am of my own surroundings. I resolved to go the library to find me some Colorado field guides. I'm not in Arroyo Seco anymore and I have to remind myself that I won't be able to identify Pitkin County's oldest crow like I can in my home county. I introduced myself and he said his name was Roger. Aspen High, class of '62. He saw me looking at his gun and asked if I wanted to shoot it. I declined saying I wasn't a fan. Roger said, "Wait till you lose five horses in one weekend to a mountain lion. Might change your mind."

I asked: "You can shoot a cougar?"

"Bet you're ass I can."

We shook hands. He had a hand like a plate. I felt like I was talking to all of rural Colorado past and present distilled into one man. I became worried whether Toby and the gang would make it through the night. Roger read my mind and muttered under his breath, "they'll be all right." As I write this, It's almost midnight and I haven't heard anything out of the ordinary outside.

* * *

In the morning, I woke before the sun. I made coffee, ate toast. My eyes opened after a bad dream at exactly five to five. My mind was racing, my belly growled, my bones ached. I had no choice but to get up and eat and drink. The dream that woke me had me momentarily forget about the mountain lion and the horses. I was sipping my coffee, black. The dream concerned the reenactment of a distant childhood memory.

I don't know why, but it was around the time I was ten or eleven. Thus far the happiest days of my life. Things just seemed right at that age, and it was my dream that brought that visceral feeling back. The dream went sideways at the memory of a childhood friend. Nothing bad happened to him in the dream, but for some reason I felt such a profound melancholy over the passage of time and the irreversibility of growing older. We were such great friends then, but that is no longer the case. Hasn't been for the past fifteen years. I am not the same person as I was one minute, or second ago. The biological clock ticks until it doesn't. I will never be the person I was nor will I be in that exact place. I will never again play soccer against kids on weekends in the Spring before school let out for summer. Who were those people in my life then? I look back at those times that appear in my dreams, random vignettes of innocent times past. I took the present for granted then, am I still?

I drank my coffee thinking these thoughts. I ate my toast. I took my time with both, watching the black of night through the kitchen's big south facing windows. To the east a sliver of grey predawn light appeared in the cold clear night. I continued drinking coffee until first light and only then thought myself brave enough to check on the horses. I put on a big ski jacket, boots and went outside. The dew on the grass had frosted and I thought to myself winter would soon be here. I took my time walking over to the barn.

I got to the horse corral and walked around to the barn's flank to enter a rear door. Inside, I saw the horses. All were there except Toby. I went back outside and around the barn's perimeter a few times to search. Sure enough on the barn's north west side I saw paw prints chilled in mud close to frozen. Lots of them shooting off in spasmodic directions. Blood smear. I tried following a set into the forest soon losing their trail. I had a strange feeling of being watched as I looked around the forest. No luck.

Back at the house, I saw Roger's kitchen light on across the road. I went over to his front door and knocked. He let me in. We sat at his dining room table and drank coffee. I could drink coffee all day long. Roger had a look in his eye that said failure. I knew just by looking at him that he'd had a hard night. He said he'd heard commotion around half past two and promptly went outside with a floodlight and his shotgun. He first went to the barn and found the horses were out in the corral running scared. Wild eyed. He'd spotted the mountain lion dragging old Toby from the corral.

"I was too late," he said. "Saw the cat with Toby's neck in his mouth. The thing clawed June too. I shot my gun and the cat fled back in the bush. I stayed there by the corral for a good couple hours doin' what I could to settle the horses." How I didn't hear the shotgun, I do not know.

"I just saw the horses, they looked fine," I said.

"You didn't take a good long look then. I bandaged June pretty good."

"Where's Toby?"

"Stayed up all night, buried him out in the bush. Got a graveyard back there. Dogs and horses." Roger looked defeated. "A tough, mean old horse, Toby. But a good horse."

I had only taken a moment's glance to see if the horses were all there and the light was poor in the barn. It was midmorning before I left Roger's. I stopped by the barn again and sure enough there was June. Bandaged and withdrawn. Together the horses stood as if to protect her. Nosing her for compassion and support.

I returned to my house and then my bed. I laid there until lunch, thinking, thinking, thinking some more. Praying for an hour of sleep. I gave up. I drank yet more coffee and ate a banana. My phone buzzed on the kitchen counter and there was a message from Norman asking me to call him as soon as possible. It was a one way conversation. I had another story to do "and could you come in before four?" I showered, threw on some clothes and ran out the door. On my way out, I saw Roger looking at me from his kitchen window. Standing there, despondent.

* * *

I arrived in Aspen, quarter to four. Norman was on his way out and invited me to join him. We went to a pub and had hamburgers and beer. Norman said his boss used to take him out for beers when he was my age.

"Back then I was writing the sports page for the Little Rock Gazette...what's wrong? You seem distant." I was thinking about Toby.

"Nothing," I said. "You were saying?"

"Second tier paper in a two tier market. Difference between then and now was we'd by now be drunk."

"What's stopping us?" Norman looked at me, smiled. When the waitress came he ordered more beer. Direct action, no legislation required. When the beers arrived, we drank them and ate more of our hamburgers, grunting while we chewed as men do. I wanted to know how Norman ended up in Aspen.

"It wasn't for the skiing," he said.

"What was it then?"

"In Arkansas, we never skied as you can imagine. While I was in Little Rock, I would cross paths from time to time with a girl about my age, selling advertisements for a glossy state magazine. All of us in the city's publishing industry would go to the same bars on weekends, and that was when I first met Maria."

"And you followed Maria to Aspen?"

"I did. She grew up here and wanted to return after working long hours on Clinton's governor campaign. They were classmates at Yale."

"No kiddin'. She still around?"

"She is."

"You know Norm, I couldn't help but see some of the photos in your office when we met last time. You and Clay Felker, Gloria Steinem, at the White House with Jimmy Carter. Was New York after Little Rock?"

"Yes and before I came to Aspen. Felker was my mentor. Our nation's best editor you ask me. It's true...Back East, I was on the fast track for a big career but I gave it all up. Maria, she came to Manhattan for a while working for Life. She wanted to come home to Aspen and settle. And I was absolutely head over heels for Maria. Coming here, best decision I ever made. Still have yet to ski."

"You never regretted leaving Manhattan?"

"Not the least bit. Meko, I think it's time we talk more about your goals."

"Sure."

"Well, what are they?"

"In journalism?"

"Yeah."

"Well, the big time. I want to be in the Times magazine, Esquire, GQ, all that. Optioning my stories to Hollywood. Turning stories into books."

"Course you do. Long form narrative, journalism's holy grail."

"Exactly."

"But you have no clue how to get there."

"None at all."

"And you're aware the market for long form writing is shrinking."

"I am."

"So why punish yourself? Why not settle into a smaller market, write good honest stories about the community, find a girl and be fine with it."

"Well, because. I think it's like giving up if I do that. I'd feel like a failure. No offence."

"None taken. I understand completely what you're saying. It's a choice. And you know, I can help you get there."

"You can? How?"

"You don't think I don't have any friends left in New York? Meko remember, in life, a lot of getting what you want is who you know, not what you know. The Chung piece you're working on. You play your cards right with that one, I'm sure it'll open doors."

"You think I should keep going on it?"

"I do. What about that Syndicate thing you brought up. Any meat on the bone?"

"Dunno. Haven't made much progress there. You're serious though about...you know, New York and such?"

"You think I'd lie to you?"

"No, it's just—"

"Hard to believe, I know. Trust me. Anyway, about the Syndicate..."

"Well what I know is there may be a connection between Native Reservations and the Sinaloa. You ever hear about that? Sound familiar?"

"Vaguely. Lots of rumour, hearsay. Pardon me for asking, but you have some Native blood?"

"I do."

"Maybe you could use that connection to your advantage. Find out more. Get your nose closer to where other reporters can't. Maybe there's something there. Maybe there's a real story here. A national story. Or maybe it's nothing and it'll be an enormous waste of your time. That's journalism. Never know unless you turn the rock over. You should chase this thing down." He paid our bill and we left. Norman said he really only ever went to that place to eat out. The owner, a friend of twenty-five years.

I said, "how old *are* you?"

"Old."

On our way out he said he expected me to continue with the social column to which I agreed. His phone was ringing non-stop but he was ignoring it as we walked to our vehicles. I left in my truck with a stinging ambiguity in the pit of my stomach over how next to proceed. Earlier this week, I noticed for the first time a plaque hanging on the wall behind Norman's head. It was an award for Outstanding Feature Journalism, Beauregard Norman, Reporter, New York Herald Tribune. I needed rest before thinking about how next to tackle this damn Chung story.

* * *

Yesterday, with my lack of sleep, the mountain lion incident, the boozy meeting with Norman and the new assignment, I resolved to find internal equilibrium in the late afternoon by grabbing my skis from my truck and skinning part way up Ajax. There was enough snow cover. I have my gear in my truck for when this impulse hits me especially living so far from town. Not that far, really, but far enough to keep ski gear on hand at all times. Ski season was only a week or so away. I needed to get on the mountain to clear my head before the inevitable crowds. I got as far as half way up before looking behind me.

What I saw was a magnificent view of the Roaring Fork Valley below. I was standing in a sea of white while the valley floor below, a painter's palette of bronze, brown, red, and yellow. A crow swirled above me as I caught my breath. I ripped the skins off my skis, threw them in my pack and adjusted my bindings for a fixed heel. I was wearing shades and the air and sun reminded me of April. I Chinese downhilled to the bottom. I have no idea how skiing as straight as possible from top to bottom on a mountain became known as Chinese downhilling. Ask anyone that has ski raced and they'll know exactly what you mean. At the base of the mountain, I was back to town. Cocktail hour and stilettos and electric cars and art galleries. It occurred to me that nowhere else that I'd skied do you drive to town to go skiing.

* * *

I called Cohen and told him I was hoping I could spend more time talking to Chung.

Cohen: "What for?"

"I need to go deeper for my story."

"You're as deep as you're going to go, bud."

I said that by going deep, that didn't mean I was looking to taint his client, just that I needed more information. Cohen wasn't really buying it and said he had to go.

"If there ever is a chance for you to go deeper with Chung and your little story, it will be with me by my client's side."

"Of course," I said. "You know, there's an opening at the end of the month, on Halloween, at the Art Museum from one of your favourite artists, you should come back then and we can figure something out."

Cohen asked who the artist was, and I told him it was a Taos area artist now in his eighties and in declining health. He must've forgotten that he told me this particular artist was one of his favourites. That he had a large collection of his paintings in his Soho apartment. Then again, he told me this only after slamming God knows how many drinks that first time I met him. What I didn't tell him was that the artist, Tim McNeil, was an old friend of my mother's. Throughout my childhood, Tim would come over to our house in Arroyo Seco for countless 'Paris in the twenties' style cocktail parties my mother was fond to host. Tim recently had been diagnosed with dementia and his heart was in rough shape. There was now a rush to show his work and also buy it up for collection purposes.

The art market can smell blood just as well as any Great White. At the mention of McNeil, Cohen just then remembered that he was going to be back in Aspen for that very exhibition. I debated whether I should tell him that I could get him a private audience with the great artist but I decided not to. It was my ace up the sleeve. At least I was aware that I could negotiate with Cohen and as luck would have it, I held a very good hand with my own connections to the New Mexican art world.

* * *

Halloween is one week away and there is plenty of talk in town about it being a special night in Aspen. I long ago abandoned dressing up and going out but perhaps this year I will. There's a private club here, the name I can't remember, that opens its doors to the public for only one night of the year on Halloween. I am not one for walled off societies, but the journalist in me wants to go to this place and be a fly on the wall. Now that I have the social column, the expectation will be that I go anyway. Did Capote, I wonder, ever feel that his own celebrity prevented him from being an anonymous journalist? I hope that doesn't ever happen to me though I think I am vastly overstating the number of chickens before they hatch on my career.

The cult of personality that some of this country's top journalists have succumbed to, a tragedy. Though partly the fault of the journalist to let that even occur in the first place, society is also to blame. Michael Lewis once said that George Plimpton became New York's tour guide the way he imbedded himself in his stories. Participatory journalism. Was that to his work's detriment? Was Plimpton prevented from do-ing certain things in his work because of his celebrity? I don't know. It's a question unanswerable. Tim McNeil is an example of an artist that just keeps going. His health is a mess on account of a wild lifestyle from his first sixty-five years, but fame and all the trappings to come with it somehow didn't affect his productivity. He's produced more work in the last twenty years than he did the preceding thirty-five.

I do think though that it is up to the individual to create opportu-nity. And yes I think that creating opportunities is akin to knowing when one rears its head. Does everything happen for a reason? I'm not so sure. My mother likes to say it does, but I think it's a mental tool she likes to use to cope with life's uncertainties and hardships. I don't know if everything happens for a reason. Probably not. But then maybe our perception of the world is entirely up to us and if my mother thinks along those lines, so be it for her. There was a comedian

I was watching on TV the other night saying he envies people who believe in heaven. There are benefits to delusion. Nice to have heaven to look forward to unlike the non-believers. I thought that was a clever observation. There are no rules on how to think. No matter how big a lawmaker's ego, you can't legislate morality. Let the cowboys ride.

* * *

I called my mother late at night and told her of my situation with Chung, his lawyer, McNeil and his upcoming exhibition. She sounded preoccupied on the other line as she always does when I try and speak with her on the phone. She said that I should talk to Tim himself and then gave me his phone number. Dogs were barking in the background and I could see in my mind's eye her four Oaxacan rescue dogs standing at her feet in the kitchen waiting for her to drop a piece of pork to the floor that otherwise would've gone into her mole. The finest I have ever tasted. Before hanging up I said she should come up to Aspen for Tim's exhibition. She laughed. "No way." I knew she would say that before I even asked, knowing how much she despised what Aspen had turned into as compared to when she used to come here in the late sixties playing the part of hippy intellectual.

* * *

Though there has been cool enough temperatures at night for snow to stick in the mountains, the days have been warm the past two weeks. Each day by two in the afternoon, sixties and sunny. The climate here is similar to what I knew growing up in Arroyo Seco. As compared to other parts of the country that I've lived in, it takes getting used to. High elevation and dry air. I do like dry air more than its counterpart but a downside is an endless need to drink water. When I exercise here, it is easy to forget how much water I am losing. The other day, I went on a run along the Rio Grande Trail after I finally got a good night's rest.

I started where the trail starts in town, on the north side by the Aspen Environmental Center. I had to drive up there of course but my plan was to do an out and back and then go have a nice meal on a patio in the late October afternoon sun. In the morning I got some work done on another story involving the implications of a proposed roundabout development. It is a testament to the power of a good rest to bear witness to the volume and quality of task I am able to perform. It was fortunate for me and the lead dog of the Aspen Environmental Center that our first encounter was on a day after I slept. Or so I initially thought. He turned out to be the same guy driving the Prius I cut off at the gas station. I parked my car at the only real visible place to do so near the entrance of the Rio Grande Trail.

I had to take a leak before I started my run and went into the woods. Midstream, I heard someone shout from behind. I turned my head to see a guy screaming at me from the road. He was sitting in his Prius. He killed the ignition and got out. I finished my business just as he made his approach. I went to the road to see what the fuss was. The angry Prius driver introduced himself. We recognized each other.

"I know that truck," he said. "You're pissing on private property." He was fuming, red in the face behind expensive looking bright red glasses and a black turtleneck.

"I'm the CEO of this place and you can't drive there and piss on our property. What's wrong with you?" I was startled for him to ask what was wrong with me. Had I not slept well, I would've punched him in the nose. But I remembered what Fitz used to tell me: "You can always tell someone to go to hell tomorrow." I told him I was new in town and it looked as though I was parked outside his organization's property lines.

He said, "what you do in town?"

"Only just visiting," I said playing dumb tourist. He eventually went on his way and I went for my run. People on the trail walked, ran, rode, in pairs, on their own, with babies. I got as far as running parallel to the airport and I started to run faster as a big jet started its takeoff. I was running alongside it and I started to sprint to try and keep up before it lifted off. I ran four miles out and then decided to turn around. I finished and was exhausted, sunburnt and dehydrated. I was dripping sweat and I changed into a different shirt and went for lunch. I left my car where it was and walked the short distance to town. Watching the jet take off alongside my run had me wondering what this town was like before there was an airport. People say that Aspen is hard to get to. It's easier than ever. Granted it's not front range close to Denver but still, there's an airport.

I found a restaurant that looked like a house. There was an open seat on the patio. The person seated at that table along with one other waved in my direction. I couldn't tell who it was but then as I walked closer I realized it was the CEO. He was inviting me to sit with him. Sitting down, he gave his name, Alec. Alec was sitting with a pretty women named Dianne who I first assumed was his wife. Wrong. It was Dianne Westcott of the Westcott Foundation. I sat with them and apologized again to Alec for my behaviour. He waved it aside. I noticed they were drinking cocktails. He asked my name I said I had a confession to make that I wasn't just a tourist but only just moved here in the past few weeks. I told Alec and Dianne that I was freelancing for the Herald. Alec knew of my work. He said he liked my writing. I ordered a pitcher of water. They had just ordered food and said I should get my order in quick. I hadn't even looked at the menu but Alec said there was no need: "Order the crispy chicken sandwich," he said.

Dianne: "Thank you for coming to my fundraiser the other night. What's your next story?"

"Halloween story, and an add-on to the Chung piece."

"There's more to the story?"

"Yes, but how much of it is accurate, I don't know."

Alec: "What can you tell us?"

"I don't talk about my stories while working on them."

Dianne: "Why not?"

"Then I lose interest in them."

Alec: "So be it. Meko are you going out and about for Halloween?"

"I am and will be writing a column about it all. Got another person to take photos."

"Did you take that over from Kim?"

"Until I leave town or she comes back from mat leave."

"Well, keep an eye out for my daughter will you?"

I laughed. "Why is that?"

"She'll be taking your photos."

"Alyssa's your daughter?"

"She is. You don't mind do you?"

"Looking after her?"

"Yeah."

"You think that's necessary?"

"She likes to have...fun. I worry. I'm a father, you wouldn't understand."

Alec grabbed his phone and showed me her Instagram account. The photos were racy.

"Popsugarasspen? I'm gonna tease her about this," I said. The photos were of her on sailboats in warm climates, at college football games, with groups of girls, at music festivals. In each photo there was a red solo cup in her hand, she was smiling, wearing revealing clothes. She liked to have fun with her girlfriends. They all looked the same. Each of her photos had a minimum of four hundred likes and artful little captions. Poetic little stanzas about being in the moment, living wild and free, that kind of thing. She was telling her story to the world, the story that she wanted to project. Her generation, of which I suppose I am a part of, feels so alien. I am unlike so many of my peers but I can appreciate the way people like Alyssa tell their own stories.

"She's taking a year off from college to live here with me in Aspen. She has a godfather here too. Her mother lives in Atlanta."

I told Alec I would look out for her. I thought it strange that he was placing this kind of responsibility on a guy he only an hour ago caught pissing on his employer's property. The conversation turned to Dianne's foundation and I became bored. I ate my food, left a crisp bill and said I had to go. That wasn't the case but I was done sitting there. To me, it looked like those two were in for a few more rounds and a big lunch.

Lyons wanted to drink wine later in the evening. She said to come to her place and could I stay the night? Yes I could, I told her. When I got to her place she was looking marvellous in an outfit perfect for Aspen. Chic high country. I became even more attracted to her and we sat on her couch drinking cheap Malbec I bought at a gas station. The conversation was all over the place. Art, skiing, Where We Are In Life, family stuff, everything. We finished the bottle and she opened another she made with friends at a U-Brew place. We took alternate swigs and sat closer to one another. She was asking me what I had planned for the weekend. I had nothing planned while she was going to Los Angeles for a sailing trip with friends around Catalina.

She lapsed into a story about one of her friends having difficulty figuring out her plane ticket. When she said the name Eve my mouth went dry. Scrambling, and hoping she didn't read my body language, I blurted out that I knew her. But I didn't say anymore and changed the subject. Lyons asked if I wanted to smoke a joint and I said no thanks. She lit up anyway and closed her eyes after a few hits. She put her head on my chest and we just sat there for a while.

They must know that I was seeing them both, how could they not? But then why was I seated where I was? Lyons must not care, or simply not know. I found it arousing to think that in liberal Aspen, the confines of a relationship were...loose. By the same token I began to wonder how many other guys had been seated this week on this couch. It started to make my head hurt thinking about it. I needed air. I needed to go. Lyons didn't protest my leaving and said she was tired anyway and going to sleep. I kissed her and said goodbye and she pulled me in for more. I left around midnight and drove down to the horse farm. I was looking to see if there was any sign of the mountain lion but my untrained eye was hopeless. The wine didn't help.

* * *

The days of Independence Pass remaining open were numbered. I wanted to drive over it once more and visit an old family friend down by South Fork. Early the next morning I left. Overnight, there had been a surprise snow fall. When I left Aspen at seven, there was a foot of it and no clouds in the sky. Beautiful. I was worried about the roads over the pass. I drove slowly and made it over, guessing on Monday the state would close the road for good. I stopped at the top and went for a brief walk out to an overlook. Sawatch Rockies as far as the eye could see. Cloudless skies, snow capped peaks. It was below freezing up there and I started to shiver with my light fall jacket on. I drove down to the other side taking my time. When I got to Twin Lakes I was kicking myself for not thinking to bring my skates. The ice had set without fault and someone had already cleared a nice little hockey rink. Later in the day there would be a good game of shinny to play without me there for it. But a visit to Stan was worth forgoing playing some puck.

Driving south with a view to the east of the Sangre de Cristo range is a sight that never will get old for me. Perhaps on my way home I would detour over from Stan's little ranch near South Fork to the Great Sand Dunes. I hadn't been there in years. I recall going there as a thirteen year old thinking I was on another planet as I walked through the dunes with my mother and twin sister cousins on dad's side. I haven't seen those cousins since. They moved shortly after our dunes experience to Rhode Island. Mom told me one of them is in Manhattan working in finance, the other helps out a family business of custom made sailboats.

The drive south on the two-eighty-five went quick and by noon I was trying to remember which road to turn off for Stan's place. His is not a big ranch. Stan and I share similar, convoluted heritage. His Native roots are of the Navajo nation. He came from nothing and married into a wealthy family but chose to stay very involved in Native affairs across the Southwest. His wife's family sold off the majority of the land to neighbours and what now remains is a little house shrouded by cottonwoods with a clear view of the Sangres. Stan lives alone, he and his wife separated two years ago. She left him to try living in Denver in hopes of "urban renewal."

I took three wrong turns and then I saw the fence post with an old boot on top. I knew from childhood memories, that was the turn. The little house built sometime in the eighteen eighties was the same as I remembered it from the last time I visited years ago. Stan had done interior remodelling through the years but the plumbing and foundation was original. My guess is that it would need replacing soon and hopefully Stan would have the energy to do so. The condition he suffers from, Trigeminal Neuralgia, makes his life difficult. I can understand his desire to live in warmer climates to help with the pain. Why I hadn't bothered to make visits between then and now, I don't know.

I was never a fan of Stan's estranged wife. In my defence, I was moving from town to town across the west. But here I was and there was Stan's transit van he takes everywhere camping, parked out front. He outfitted the back of it such that one could live in the damn thing and feel like it was a Holiday Inn. Last winter he lived in it for close to two months out near Tucson before making his way back to Colorado.

Stan greeted me warmly, offering beer and meat off his barbecue. The pain comes in unpredictable waves and thankfully I caught him at a time when he was in comfort. When the pain comes, he says he can't face the world. I told him around five that I needed to exercise after a day in the car and he suggested I go run up a nearby butte. That's what I did and when I got back to his place, he had prepared veal ossobuco for us. He shot the animal himself and there was nothing else I could've asked for. Mashed potatoes and lentils on the side with a bottle of Bordeaux. Stan was telling me about his latest procedure down in Arizona to help him deal with his condition. An ex-girlfriend from before his marriage introduced him to top docs at a neurological institute in Phoenix. Five years ago he had four millimetres of his trigeminal nerve singed by a gamma knife. This past September he had the same procedure. In between, there had been considerable advancements in the medical field to address what he calls his "truly fucked up situation."

We ate and drank and our spirits were high. I was telling him about my time in Aspen and he thought it was fairly entertaining, the whole scene. We played cribbage like we always do until two, three in the morning before I said I needed to sleep. I like to think I am a skilled cribbage player but try as I might, Stan always wins our last game.

I woke early Sunday morning to Stan reading the New York Times. He sat at a table with a view to the east of the mountains drinking black coffee, wearing frameless reading glasses. The morning sun blasted through the windows forcing him to squint. Just as I walked in his toast popped. I buttered it for him and he didn't know I was even in the room until I came within his peripheral vision. He said there was more coffee in the pot over by the kitchen sink. There was bread out and I put some in the toaster and sat down to drink my coffee at the table while Stan read.

After a while he laughed and put the paper down on the table saying there was "no good news anymore." He wanted to know if I could hopefully write better than what he was reading in the nation's paper of record. I said I tried my best. He asked, "Do you have any of your stuff for me to see?" I told him I didn't but that I had a few pages of a novel I had long ago abandoned in my truck. A western. He looked at me and I knew I had to get the papers. Before I did, I wanted to ask him if he knew anything about the Syndicate.

"Syndicate?" Stan asked. "What's that?"

"You ever heard of Native tribes being exploited for the legal protection reservation's have?"

"Can happen, yes."

"I think something like that is happening in Aspen."

"You know, it's funny you say that. Few years ago at a tribal meeting, there was a guy I overheard mention something like that. Darwin I think his name was."

"No kiddin'. How so?"

"From the Arapaho. He wouldn't stop complainin' that they weren't getting their fair share."

"Fair share of what?"

"I can't remember. Had something to do with a foundation not holding up their end of a deal."

"No shit."

"Yeah. Never know with foundations. So easy for them to remain opaque and do all kinds of shit behind closed doors, if you know what I mean. You want, I could track him down for ya?"

"Stan that would be so helpful. Rumour in Aspen is there's a connection with the Sinaloa about selling imported contraband. I don't know, it's all really hazy right now. No one wants to talk about it, but people seem to be aware of it."

"Wouldn't be surprised if our peoples have somehow been bilked. Nothing new there. I'll track him down for you. Might be helpful."

"Thanks."

"No problem. Now, go get those papers. I want to read what you got."

Later that morning after returning from a walk along an old fence line, Stan said he'd finished reading my stuff and wondered if I'd like to hear his thoughts. "Sure," I said. This would be the last thing before me leaving to visit the Dunes. Stan liked my story concept but he said the writing needed work. The style and structure, both good, but there was an "honesty lacking." I know how much of a reader Stan is, and I also know he studied comparative literature at the University of Wyoming. I respect his opinion. I said to him that I was having trouble finding my voice as distinct from those writers I read and admire. "Tell me a story," he said. When I asked why, he got to the point: if you can tell a good story verbally, there is something there that is unique to be found on the page. Unique to yourself. He encouraged me to continue the project. "If for no other reason than to come up with a better idea for a story while you're writing it." We ate the rest of the veal wrapped in corn tortillas for lunch before I left. Stan stood there on his front step looking out at me as I drove off.

* * *

It was mid-afternoon when I got to the Dunes and there was only a few other cars in the parking lot. The weather was still clear and I started my walk up the mounds of sand. I could see others way up ahead but the wind quickly obscured their tracks. There was no trail, no signage, nothing but a direction to walk in. It took me two hours to summit the highest dune. The sand is difficult to hike through, and I was taking more photos than necessary. The cerulean sky, beige sand and occasional snow patch; It was like another planet. Just like when I visited as a teenager.

Other people I could see were parking their cars in the lot and making their way in my direction from miles away. They looked like ants as they moved across the sand. The mountains of which the dunes are apart had storm clouds shrouding snow capped peaks. My boots were filled with sand and I was thirsty not having water with me. When I got back to my truck, I took my shoes off and put on a pair of Birkenstocks. I left in the early evening traveling north. I stopped in Buena Vista for Mexican food before making the final push over the pass to Aspen.

When I got to Twin Lakes, the driver of a white Chevy Suburban didn't bother to look to see if I was coming. He turned out from a resort hotel onto the road, I swerved and honked. When I lifted my hand off the horn, it didn't stop. There was nothing I could think to do to fix it and so I just kept driving with my truck horn blaring on the tailgate of the Suburban. The entire drive up and down the pass, my horn blasted in the key of G. The guy in front of me must've thought I was insane. I was worried that the thing would never stop. What would I do when I got back to Aspen? To my relief and the guy driving the Suburban, the windy roads had me reefing on the steering wheel. Reefing the wheel fixed the problem. The Suburban never pulled over to let me pass. Sure enough, the next day I heard on the radio the pass was closed for the season. And my lead to Darwin? Visiting Stan, the best thing I've done in a while.

* * *

The end of October fell on a Tuesday, which meant the weekend leading up to it was for when adults celebrated their version of Halloween. I went to the party to take photos for my now weekly column. Before that, I attended Tim's opening at the museum. And before that I met Cohen for lunch. Sitting across from us was Dianne and Alec. The setting was an haute cuisine Italian place on Hopkins. When I saw Alec holding Dianne's hand, I knew then that there was more to their relationship. They waved at me and I waved back and then Cohen asked who they were. When I told him, he looked over his shoulder and then back at me excited. "That's Dianne Westcott?" Cohen pulled her profile up on his phone from the foundation's website. A lawyer he knew used to hire his firm all the time to do work for the foundation.

Cohen: "Ted Gaffney is his name and I still on occasion do work for him."

"No kidding, I met Ted the other day and his wife. What kind of work?"

"My firm makes that colossal of a foundation appear legal."

"What kind of foundation again?"

"All to do with Indian economic development stuff." My head popped with questions but Cohen closed his eyes.

"You simply can't know anymore," he said.

The real reason of course for our lunch was to discuss, as Cohen liked to say, the "media strategy" for his client Won Seok Chung. I don't think of what I do as someone else's media strategy and told Cohen as much.

Eventually he agreed to let me speak again to his client still behind bars. I asked how he was doing in there, Cohen said he was doing fine. When I brought up the subject of Tim McNeil, Cohen perked right up. The plan we finally agreed on was: after lunch we would visit Won Seok and from there go to the museum early to have drinks with Mc-Neil before his opening. Alec saw us getting up to leave and to my slight embarrassment he blurted from across the restaurant "to watch for Alyssa tonight." I smiled without reply and briskly walked out.

Cohen asked outside who Alyssa was and I told him it was his college aged daughter living with him in Aspen. Cohen asked why he said that in the restaurant. All I could say to him was that according to her father, she was "on the loose."

* * *

We found Won Seok Chung busy playing gin rummy with a fellow inmate. We didn't have long to visit with him so I began asking my questions. I expected him to look ragged and tired but on the contrary, he looked rested and fit. He explained his good health to me as a result of "Won Seok time" in the jail cell, and the voluminous reading he'd been doing. He'd said he'd taken advantage of the jail's library and had been reading the poetry of Yeats "to distraction." I tried but failed not to laugh. When I began my line of inquiry, I cut right to the chase. I asked him point blank whether the rumour was true.

Chung: "What rumour?"

"You were trying to find a stash of cash?"

"Cash for?"

"The deal that went sideways"

"Involving?"

"Erikson, a friend of your father's, and the sheriff." Chung paused a beat.

"Very good," he said.

Cohen was indignant over what had just been said. But the heavy lunch with wine did wonders to muzzle him. I knew that I wasn't going to get much else from Chung. What Chung had just said was a fabulous addition I could now make to my amended story. Won Seok had only one more thing to say to me before Cohen started ushering me out. "You must know Pete," he said with a wry smile.

I was lucky to have the Tim McNeil connection as a way to placate Cohen for the rest of my time with him. He said he needed another drink after the jail scene. We went to a bar until it was time to head over to the museum. In an hour, Cohen had four whiskeys to my one. I don't know what was eating him up so much but after whiskey number three, he volunteered the information himself.

His wife wanted a divorce. She was the main bread winner and he was soon to be cut off from her credit cards. She made him sign a prenup twenty years ago when they got married. Before his wife could freeze his accounts, he wanted to purchase all the McNeil he could. He knew of a guy in Florida who would gladly pay a premium for the work so as to not have to leave his Vero Beach compound. A retired baseball player who's Yale MFA educated wife was buying up a collection for her own gallery. It was a convoluted story but isn't every art market story? That's what mom taught me. In the art world, the rational man modelled in modern economics does not exist.

* * *

We met Tim at the museum. Cohen was visibly drunk. I wasn't sure if Tim would remember me but he did. He said he could spot a Torres from a mile away. We hugged and I introduced Cohen and then Cohen left to the restroom. In the time he was gone, Tim and I caught up. He wanted to know how I was doing in this "shit hole of a town." I said I was managing. "How long you gonna last? I thought by now you'd be somewhere out in the southwest camping."

I took that as a compliment and only then for the first time did I realize that me being in Aspen was against my character. Since graduating Dartmouth, I'd lived in Red Lodge Montana, Mendocino California, Driggs Idaho, Pacific City Oregon, Fredericksburg Texas, Flagstaff Arizona (my only city experience) and of course Arroyo Seco. I left New England as soon as I finished my last exam and never looked back. Parts of New Hampshire I did like, as with Vermont, but too old and cold and settled in its ways over there.

Tim knew that I had a buyer with me and I said to just give him some of his plein air studies. That this guy will pay way above market for those pieces done as exercise. Tim said he had a few and that he would gladly if it meant helping me out. I said it would, that he was the lawyer for the guy who I was writing about for the paper here. Tim cut me off and asked angrily why I wasn't writing fiction. I told him I needed to pay the bills. Tim said I should just teach skiing and write my fiction.

The opening went well and Tim did his thing to please the crowd. I ducked out around eight and assured Cohen he had first look on a rare plein air collection. I was sick of this guy and after he asked if he could "get anything in writing," I left the museum to find a place to change into my Halloween costume. I was going as a mariachi singer.

* * *

I found Alyssa right away after I ducked into a public restroom to switch into my costume. I walked out of there looking like I'd just arrived from Playa Del Carmen. The Halloween party was at a place normally frequented by older women on the prowl. The Elk Club. Every year for Halloween the place opened for the public. Alyssa was dressed as slutty tinker bell with a camera. She was with friends and they were all doing shots at the bar and they all looked college aged and all were dressed as sorority cheerleaders. I didn't know if I should approach. I walked up to the same bar and took a few photos of the bartender in a Kleenex box costume. He was doing some flashy stuff with the bottles which I thought perfect for the story.

One of Alyssa's friends saw me taking photos and shoved a shot of vodka toward me. The music was loud, she was drunk and impressed with my camera. I slugged the shot. Her name was Heather and she said to come drink with her and her friends. I photographed them all together posing for my camera. I said I was going to publish these for next week's Herald and asked for their names. They all immediately told me before asking what day exactly they would appear in the paper. When they finished giving their names, Alyssa grabbed me by the arm and pulled me toward a booth. She asked why I was taking photos. I told her I didn't know if she was going to be here. That she hadn't bothered to reply to my message.

Alyssa said, "that's because I was pissed you met my dad."

"Wasn't exactly my choice."

"True. But he said you did agree to be my chaperone."

"Only way I could get him to stop asking."

"When did you even meet him?"

"Well, we met on a patio for lunch one day. He was with Dianne—"

"He said you cut him off at the gas station and then found you pissing on his building."

"What? It wasn't on his building for chrissake...I was in the—"

"Whatever. I don't need supervision. Got it?"

"You're a big girl now. You can make your own decisions."

"Oh, fuck off. Anyway, I took all the photos you'll need."

"Thanks. Wanna let me know next time if you're gonna show?"

"You do your job, I'll do mine."

"That's how you want it fine."

"By the way, nice camera. You know you only need an iPhone nowadays. Just have to know how to use it."

With that, she turned around and I could've sworn she twerked her butt up in my direction. I was incapable of not following her as she walked to the other side of the bar presumably to go out for a smoke on the patio. She did exactly that and I lit a cigarette she produced from no name packaging. I don't smoke and never have a lighter on me but the costume I was wearing happened to have one in the front pocket. Lyons was loaning me the costume from a friend of hers. Alyssa let me have a couple drags which put me into a coughing fit. My lungs, unused to heat and smoke. But this stuff was strong.

"What is that?"

"Private label, can't find this tobacco in stores," she said.

I put her on the spot by asking what she thought of the whole Chung situation. She asked if I even knew the real story behind the break-in. I said I did know the real deal but wasn't able to put it in print. She sighed.

"How pathetic community journalism can be. Would you like to go for sushi? I'm sick of this place." I told her I could go for sushi after doing a few more interviews. I didn't see her for the next hour until I heard my name yelled from behind. "Your job is done, now let's go for sushi."

We left and she grabbed my hand, interlacing her fingers in mine. I didn't protest. She ordered spinach and tofu. We sat side by side and she whispered in my ear to not let anyone talk to her. I nodded and looked around at the busy restaurant. I didn't know a soul. She knew everyone.

I asked, "Aren't you new here?"

"Yeah, but Aspen's small. I like to go out."

We were the only ones in the restaurant dressed for Halloween. We were getting looks. Slutty tinker bell sitting beside a drunk mariachi singer.

She asked: "So, what do you know about that story?"

"Cover ups, unlikely allies, you know..."

"Specifics?"

"You think I'm just gonna tell you? What do you know, anyway?"

"You think I don't know?"

"No, I don't think you do." She looked at me silently for a beat and then said I was right, she didn't know a thing. I didn't believe her.

She said, "But could you tell me?"

"Hell no," I said. "Read about it when I sell the story to Hollywood."

"I know a guy here who used to work in Hollywood," she said.

"Doing?"

"Directing and stuff, I bet he'd like it."

My ears perked and I felt her draw me in. Did she have an innate sense of knowing what guys want for her to manipulate? I was going down valley and she was going back out on the town. I felt pangs of guilt after neglecting to text Eve back after she asked what I was doing. I didn't reply because Alyssa now had a firm hold on my heart. I had no reason to understand why that was now the case. I drove home and read a Jim Harrison novel until three in the morning before crashing to sleep. What a night.

November

Where was I? On a horse farm near Carbondale, Colorado. What was I doing? Waking up, drinking coffee and reading the day's Herald delivered by my neighbour Roger. What time was it? Not yet ten in the morning. Who did I need to talk to today? My editor, Beau Norman. My three girls: Wild Child Alyssa, Skier Eve, Southern Belle Lyons. Cohen could wait. I knew he was in town for a few more days and this morning, too hungover to talk.

I had to pay Donna November's rent. I hadn't seen much of her the past month, always doing something upstairs. The check I wrote, I hoped it would clear. I had money in my account, enough to pay rent, but did the checks I deposited a few days ago clear in time? The last thing I wanted to do was make Donna think I was in dire financial straits. While that in fact may've been true, appearances are everything and I didn't want her to kick me out thinking she wouldn't get her rent in due time.

Before I called Norman I prepared an email to him with my Halloween column. All told, underwhelming. People dressed up getting hammered. That's the story. It took me no more than half an hour to write it and then I looked through the camera's memory to pick out photos to send. I would have to go to a cafe later to send my story and the photos Alyssa had sent me. Alyssa took great shots. Maybe there is a skill learned from all her Instagramming. People like Alyssa learn to take a photo and tell a story with it. I didn't know anyone in her photos and realized that I would need names to go along with the photos. I drove toward town. As soon as I got enough reception, I called her. She answered on the third ring and guessed right away that I needed her help. She said to meet her in an hour for breakfast in Aspen.

When I got to the little diner, apparently closing for good at the end of the month, she was sitting at a booth by the window. When I sat down with my camera and a notepad, she said she was going to miss the place.

"I thought you were new here," I said.

"I am, but I can tell that this town's soul is going out the window when these little ma-pa's start closing."

"How old are you?"

She said: "how old are you?" We looked at each other and we both knew we were in our twenties so why answer. But the question I really wanted to know the answer to was who she was as a person for saying all of these interesting things.

Alyssa: "I am good looking and so therefore the assumption is I don't have to think."

"Says who?"

"Everyone except you...what you're thinking."

"Gimme some slack."

"Let's just do this, eat and then...how bout a hike?"

"Hike on hold, I have to file this today and go in to talk to Norman."

"Stays light late..."

"Okay, where?"

"Ute."

"Ute...trail?"

"You don't know?"

"Show me."

At Norman's office, I walked in to him talking on the phone. At the cafe with Alyssa, I sent him an email with the photos and story. "Nice story, even better photos," he said, getting off the phone.

"Thanks."

"How's our Korean Confidential story coming?"

"I'm getting access to Chung because I happened to have direct contact with an artist who's work is featured prominently in Chung's lawyer's friend's wife's gallery in Miami."

"Come again?"

"You heard me. Not only that, I'm waiting to hear from an Arapaho about a possible connection between his tribe being screwed over by the Westcott Foundation."

"Come again?"

"Long story how I found the lead, but anyway, I'm still waiting to hear from him. Was supposed to call last week. Never heard."

"Well, however you're going about it, I need a story before Thanksgiving. I think that would play well with the crowds in town."

I left his office with an hour left before I was to meet Alyssa. I went to a cafe and called Lyons. She asked how my night went. Well, I said. She said she was thinking of coming but then decided to stay in. Pity, I said. She asked if I wanted to come over for dinner tonight and drink some more wine. I said I'd be there at seven. The phone conversation ended and I walked over to the library to see Eve. She was greeting visitors at the front and when she saw me coming through the front doors, she turned and walked away. I ran after her, wondering what was wrong. She must've seen me last night or maybe a friend of hers did. Aspen is small. I caught up with her just as she was going through a door marked "employees only." She whirled around angrily to ask why I didn't call her last night.

"And who was the teenager?"

"She's not a teenager," I said, stupidly.

"She's like twenty, give me a break. Has a rich dad and a fake ID."

I wasn't going to fight this. "I know, you're right. Long story, but I met her father and she's a freelancer for the Herald. The work would help her resume for what she was studying."

Eve glared, looking for a tell. None came from me. She softened. We hugged and then I asked her if she would like to do something this weekend.

She asked: "What about tonight?"

"Busy."

"Oh, what you up to?"

"Donna my landlord is having me up to her's for dinner, I should go because we haven't had a chance to get to know one another."

"Have fun with...Donna."

"You actually think?"

"I don't know about you."

"Why don't we go for a bike ride tomorrow? If it's not too cold?"

"Bike's in the shop. Let's go hiking...been up Ute yet?"

"No, where's that?"

We hugged, I kissed her and then I left to drive over to the Ute trail.

Alyssa was late. I waited in my truck listening to KDNK. Blues. Paul Butterfield. Alyssa pulled up beside me and I asked her to come in and listen. Seventies live album from Chicago start to finish. I figured she wouldn't like it. But no, she knew the label it was on.

We huffed it up the steep trail on the east side of Aspen Mountain. We considered walking all the way to the top of the mountain after arriving to the top of the trail. Alyssa was in shape to do that and so was I but we decided to turn around. I led the way down, she the way up. At the bottom, we were wet with sweat and thirsty for water. We shared a granola bar in my truck and Alyssa slid into the front seat and started kissing me. I was caught off guard. I pulled back and looked into her eyes. She had a look that said "what are we waiting for." Lots to wait for was what I was thinking but did not say. She pulled me in again. We continued making out in my truck and then I stopped. I wasn't ready for this to happen.

"Am I not pretty enough?"

"That's not why at all."

"Then what is it?"

"Too fast, good things take time."

"Not what is it, who is it, I meant"

"There isn't another person," I said. We stopped and then she returned to her car. I told her I would like to see her again. She was miffed.

"When?"

"We'll figure something out"

"Okay..."

We left each other and while driving the short distance back to town I called Lyons.

"Hey, I'm ready now to meet, can you?"

"Come to my place, we can drink wine and then go for dinner." Lyons was at the door, wearing yoga pants and a sports bra.

I asked, "You busy?"

"Well, I'm not going to put my life on hold just because you're ready...I'm doing Bikram."

"Can I watch?"

"Only if you do it with me."

"I'll need guidance."

I took my pants and shirt off and we started doing Bikram. Never having done it, I didn't know right from wrong. What I did know was that the moves she was making were...provocative. I was having trouble concentrating, staying in pose. The music she had on was new-age stuff, ambient noises and whale calls. Lit candles all over her living room. Old bird cages hung as interior decoration. She said I needed to finish by going into a deep child's pose. I didn't know what that was. She demonstrated.

Me: "What's deep and what isn't?"

"I want you to put both your hands on my lower back and press gently but firmly down. Listen to how I breath and exhale." I followed orders and stooped low enough to kiss the back of her neck. She breathed a deep breath and stayed in child's pose.

"Do that again," she said. I did, and then she said it was my turn. I got into the pose and she sat on my lower back. I was deep in child's pose and didn't even notice her right arm come around to pinch my member. I almost bucked her off my back. She laughed. When she got off, I took her over to the couch. I was trying to take her bra off. She stopped me.

"Not yet," she said.

"When?"

"I don't know. I don't even know you. Good things take time."
Tough pill to swallow. But I did.

I asked, "Are we going to dinner tonight?"

"Yes! I have a reservation."

"Where?"

"Nicest place in town."

"You know the bartender?"

"No. You are taking me and you are paying for our meals. You
think I'd let you make love to me without taking me to dinner first?"

* * *

We arrived late to our reservation. The restaurant, a classic Aspen
joint around forever. I opened the menu and saw the prices and took a
deep breath. Lyons saw my body language and said she was only kidding. That we were going to eat at the bar. Our waitress I later learned,
a friend. She had the table set aside to see how I would react to the
prospect of paying a couple months earnings for a plate of food. Inside
joke among friends. She gave us our dessert on the house. My burger
and her chef's salad were given to us at discount. I tipped mightily. We
returned to her place and resumed Bikram by Lyons. The candles
burned low, the bird cages cast long spooky shadows on her walls and I
lost track of where I was, what I was doing. Yet still, she denied our
making love. I was ravenous but I could wait.

In the morning I felt disoriented, confused. What was I doing with
Lyons, Alyssa, and Eve? This couldn't last. I have a good heart and I
was feeling ill about it all. Walking from her door to my vehicle, I felt
an urge to get to work. When in doubt, hard work cures all that ails. I
left her place with renewed dedication toward my work as a journalist.
The girl situation would work itself out, that was my hope. I still had a
weekend filled with plans with Eve, but I promised myself I would
start next week ready to grind it out.

* * *

Walking up the Ute trail again, this time with Eve, we spoke of the ski season ahead. I was feeling the money pinch again after paying rent. When she brought up her client visiting from Brazil, I jumped at the opportunity to ask if she could use my help with instruction. I liked Eve in particular because given that she is a ski instructor, she had no qualms about me subverting the system and doing private lessons. What was news to me, was her explaining the way the company that owns all four of Aspen, Highlands, Buttermilk and Snowmass operates the ski school.

The fee for a private lesson is about a thousand bucks. Of the one thousand, about one hundred goes into the instructor's pocket. Eve is a level three professional ski instructor, the highest she can go, and the company completely owns her earning power. Of course, the company would say, if it weren't for us you wouldn't have a job, a venue, anything. True, but taking that much of the fee to me seems unfair. Eve said the money for her is in tips.

Her mention of tips reminded me of a thirty year plus veteran of Wall Street I had a beer with the other day. He ran trading businesses at three different banks and when we talked about income inequality, he laughed. He said that on Wall Street, the norm is to earn a mere one or two percentage points on the profits you earn from trading as an annual bonus. A banker's salary is a joke to try and live on in Manhattan. He said some years he earned fifty million in trading profits but only kept pre-tax one mil as a bonus. After tax, around six hundred thousand. Six hundred thousand is lots of money but compared to fifty million? Indentured labour.

The bonus in ski instruction of course is the tip money. I asked if her Brazilian client was a tipper, and she said that he was but not "willy nilly." Results based. That rang true for me and I was eager to reach out. To my surprise however, the Brazilian emailed me first. Eve gave him my email and a couple days later I woke up to see a message from one Gabriel Coutinho. He asked me if I could instruct his daughters, aged fourteen and twelve for three to four weeks, starting the second week of December. I said sure, let's circle back on this in a few weeks.

Eve told me later the Coutinho family comes to Aspen every other year, each time wearing matching Prada ski outfits. That got me worried. Eve laughed saying they were good people, don't worry. I didn't want to count my chickens, but the thought of thousands in my bank account for a few weeks work went a long way to easing my financial anxieties. I took Eve out and no we didn't eat at a fancy restaurant, she wouldn't allow for that. We ate at a cheap barbecue place on the way out of town. I had brisket and white bread and she had a pulled pork sandwich. She said, "You can spend money on me after Christmas, dear."

* * *

With a couple weeks until Thanksgiving, I had plenty of time to polish the Chung piece. But I felt completely over it. At times I considered throwing in the towel. But I wouldn't let myself give in. I knew it was the future instructing income that was the culprit. All this work for maybe a hundred bucks once the story was published? Indentured labour. Not even the goals I discussed with Norman were motivating. At least I found it interesting work and informing to my fiction writing.

After my visit with Stan, I decided to continue the stagnant novel I started over a year ago. A western. I changed the setting from Utah to old Colorado. I tend to get stuck on thinking it's cliché. I don't care. I just want to write the story wherever my creative impulse takes it. Just do the work. Get the words down. The rest will follow. Late at night or first thing in the morning is my writing time for both fiction and journalism. Since my visit with Stan, I've devoted more of my juices to fiction. Perhaps I will find more under-the-table clients to instruct this ski season, freeing me to write only fiction. Reading the paper is good

enough I think to inform my stories of social realism. Tom Wolfe es-
sayed about the importance and lost opportunity for American writers
turning their backs on what was happening right before their eyes. I
think he's right and I want to keep my fiction grounded in scene-by-
scene construction, extensive use of dialogue, and so on. Cerebral finger painting is just not for me.

* * *

Later that week I met with Cohen again. He was flying back to La-
Guardia the next day and this would be the last time before Thanksgiving for him in town. He said someone else was going to take over after.
He needed a vacation. I wanted to squeeze the most out of this meeting and demanded we see Won Seok in jail. Cohen didn't object. We
went for our visit after going for lunch in town. Cohen paid, saying I
had no idea how grateful he was that I finagled him the plein airs from
McNeil. I wanted him to tell me more about the situation in Miami
and after some prodding, he finally gave in. He said he was going to
pay big bucks to ensure the safe transit of the works from Aspen to
South Florida. I asked him if he knew how much he should be selling
the art for. He said he was just going to take what was offered.

"So it was your wife that is now divorcing you that showed you
art?"

"Entirely, my thing is baseball."

"Does your wife know you have the plein air pieces?"

"No. And don't tell her if she asks."

"She knows who I am?"

"No. I'm just saying that she can't know."

"And if she does find out?"

"She will demand a portion of the proceeds in our divorce. I need
all I can get."

"How much you thinking?"

"If I tell you, you're going to demand a lot more of me for fair trade."

"Try me."

"The pitcher is going to pay me half a mil for those pieces."

"You're kidding."

"No. He's newly retired, thinks he found a new hobby valuing art that his wife likes. Thinks his values will set new benchmarks."

"They could?"

"Not my problem, I just need for those paintings to arrive before Basel begins and then I get my money and my soon to be ex won't have a clue."

* * *

Won Seok Chung was sitting in his jail cell reading his Yeats. Cohen and I were still talking about the art delivery and Chung heard as much on our approach to his cell. I sat down across from him with my notebook and Cohen said he'd be right back after taking a call. Chung and I were alone to speak. I took advantage of the opportunity. I asked him to tell me what was going on. Chung said that Cohen was a very sharp lawyer and that he was successful in having his charges dropped. In a few weeks he hopefully would be airborne to Seoul. That was impressive but all I wanted to know was what actually happened and why.

In the five minutes Cohen was gone, Chung said that a close business associate of his father knows Erikson well and hosted him for one of those on stage Q and A's in Seoul. Afterward, Chung's father took a big group out for dinner. Erikson was seated next to Chung. They spoke of America and Chung brought up Aspen after having just watched Aspen Extreme. Erikson said he spent lots of time in Aspen and that if ever Chung was in the US, he should visit. They exchanged emails and for the next month, the two kept in touch. Soon, it became clear to Chung that Erikson had what he thought were feelings for him. Chung wasn't oriented that way but was so keen to enmesh himself in all things Aspen, that he went along with Erikson's flirting. Emails turned to text messages turned to hours long phone calls. For reasons unknown to Chung, Erikson's infatuation only increased the more they spoke. Chung started telling Erikson of the family businesses. It went on like this for weeks and then one day Erikson said he bought Chung plane tickets from Seoul all the way to Aspen "and could you please come stay with me?"

When Chung arrived, Erikson was nowhere to be found and the person greeting him at the Aspen airport was Pete Christopher. Pete was holding a sign that had Chung's name on it horribly misspelled. Chung followed Pete to his irrigation truck and when he saw the vehicle, that's when the question marks arose. Chung said Pete took him down to a ranch by Woody Creek and it was there he saw who he later identified as the sheriff packing up case loads of cigarettes in the back of a delivery van. They were being bought and sold without any business license. Tax free cigarettes, a big business Chung said. Pete told Chung the cigarettes were coming up from Mexico and distributed to Native American reservations across the southwest. Once on the premise of a reservation, there was much greater protection from the law to then sell to people at a discount.

So the whole racket was illegal cigarette distribution and Erikson fit into the mix because he thought cheaper cigarettes could be procured from Korea, and the Mexicans could be cut out. Erikson complemented his salary threefold by the cigarette earnings. With Korean imports, tenfold. Same with the sheriff and all the peons working for them. I asked him how Erikson came to that conclusion about the Korean cigarette business. Chung said his family wasn't only in oil and gas, but also tobacco. They invested in the business years ago and make a fortune off cigarette dividends. I was just about to ask him how the Westcott Foundation fit in, but the sound of Cohen's loafers approaching shut Chung right up. When Cohen returned, Chung and I were talking about living conditions in prison. Cohen said that Chung would soon be on his way to Korea and I acted like it was the first time I heard the news.

* * *

We left the Pitkin County jail and as we parted ways, I asked Cohen if he could spare a cigarette. Cohen shot me a glance. I knew then he knew I knew. Was Cohen also involved? He is under financial pressure right now and could probably offer a great deal of legal counsel to the players in this game. Pete was off bird hunting, perhaps Cohen was picking up his slack? Conjecture of course, but now I was intrigued. Last time I felt this way, I surprised even myself at the dedication and resolve I found to shine light on the truth. That story involved exposing land owners in eastern Montana using violence and intimidation to illegally block access across their land. Those fucking ranchers thinking they're above the law, preventing people from using public roads across their properties to recreate in the great outdoors.

* * *

Thursday morning I went straight to Norman's office and shut the door behind me. I had to let him know what I now knew. After I finished telling him about Chung's cigarette confessional, he sat back in his recliner and closed his eyes and rubbed his brow.

Norman said, "You sure about this?"

"Between Chung's newfound inner zen and his lawyer's body language over my mention of tobacco, my gut says yes. I told you about the Pete Christopher connection right?"

"I was wondering how he fit in to all this."

"I think he got involved as a hired hand to make a few extra bucks... he knows this town, and the underside of it better than Chung, Erikson, and Cohen."

"So does Sheriff Bledsoe."

"True, but how much can Bledsoe really involve himself? My bet is Pete does a lot of what Bledsoe isn't willing or capable of doing given his job title."

"Is the amount of money even worth the trouble?"

"Chung said it was the entire southwest they distribute."

"Wow. And what about the connection to Westcott?"

"Still waiting on that. Odd that I haven't heard back."

"Meko, you need to follow up on that. I remember you said the tribe tried to take the foundation to court but the lawyers got in the way?"

"Yeah...wait a minute..."

"What?"

"This could be it."

"What could be?"

"If we can somehow show evidence the Westcott Foundation is in fact providing legal protection on top of the protection provided by the reservations..."

"Then there's no way a lawyer could keep the case out of the courts."

"Like what happened in the past."

"Meko..."

"I know."

"Find that damn Arapaho!"

Norman still wanted the story by Thanksgiving and reminded me Chung was the same person who used voices in his head to explain why he broke into the house that night. Why he did that is still unclear but I am imagining it has something to do with Erikson manipulating him to do so in the matters of the heart department. What I needed was to find some sort of paper evidence to link what Chung said to me. Importation documents, evidence of the cigarettes themselves, that kind of thing. I needed to speak again with Pete Christopher but he was no longer in town. I had to find Darwin.

* * *

The event that I was responsible for covering this first week of November was a screening at the Wheeler Opera House and a reception afterward for Harry Garr. Garr, now in his eighties, made it big in the sixties as a director, writer, producer for that period of American mainstream film later deemed "New Hollywood." The film shown this week was one Garr made but never distributed. Garr moved from Los Angeles to Aspen in the early sixties after making a few bucks off an early picture about disaffiliated biker gangs. I don't know where his place is, but to my benefit, my column allowed me to set up an interview with the man himself. Garr doesn't email, nor does he have a cell phone. The day before the screening, I was told Garr was aware that I may show up to his home for an interview. I was given his home address by Norman who made it clear that I'd be in trouble if anyone found out the location of Garr's house. The man likes his privacy.

Garr's house I discovered wasn't all that far from the horse farm. Way back on a piece of land up Lake Wildcat Road in Old Snowmass. I drove there Thursday evening and was greeted by five beagles as the light of day gently faded. Garr's home had soul. Ranch house meets ski chalet circa late sixties. The beagles barked and sniffed my ankles and calves. One jumped up on me and I scratched behind her left ear. The front door of the house opened and there was Garr calling after his dogs. There was an empty pig pen on the east side of the property and a fenced field behind the house without any horses. Garr was getting old.

He waved me over, we shook hands. I introduced myself and as I did so I glanced over his right shoulder inside the eclectic house. He offered mezcal of Oaxacan provenance pouring two glasses. Just as we were about to start though he wondered if I would like a tour of the place to which I said absolutely. Garr led me through the house after first showing me around the perimeter of his property. A towering view of Capitol Peak to the southwest flush with alpen glow stopped us in our tracks, interrupting his descriptions of the surrounding vegetation.

I was nervous. Never do I get this way, but the great deal of respect that I for some reason felt toward Garr had me knotted. I had to drink the mezcal abruptly so Garr would pour me more, that was my hope. He did, and four ounces in, I was loose enough to start asking questions. Open ended type questions meant to give him the opportunity to expand. But also questions like if he'd planted his garlic yet. The little things. "Next week," he said. There were all kinds of Serrano peppers spread out on a table on his back porch. When we walked by he picked a couple up in his hand and started eating them like carrots. He offered that I could have as many as I'd like to take home. I didn't at first notice, but as he was telling me about the peppers, he also was pissing on the grass and spitting old tobacco chew. This guy was doing his own thing.

Garr wore an earth toned Carhartt jacket, leather boots and a plaid shirt with suspenders. The setting sun framed his dark skin. His whispy white hair hidden under a black gaucho style hat. He had an austere look betrayed by a Cheshire grin he liked to flash. His undistributed film was ostensibly what I came to talk about with him, but I ended up helping him around his property for a good two hours talking minimally before sitting down at his dinner table for a few bowls of homemade gazpacho. Only after we finished did we start talking. He apologized if I had to be somewhere, saying he figured he would try and get some help after he was told a young guy was coming to visit. Usually, he said, it was only beautiful young women that ever made it this far to do media with him. I recoiled at the mention of me "doing media" and he must've sensed it for he asked shortly thereafter if I was working on anything more creative. I said I was. "Good man," he said. We left it at that, and resumed our conversation about the upcoming screening. Garr didn't care one lick if the film was seen or not.

The purpose of the event was him doing a favour to an old friend involved with programming Aspen's independent film slate. We drank more mezcal and I offered to build a fire. The thing was roaring in no time with the staccato yip of a pack of coyotes in the background. Garr stopped mid sentence to listen before resuming the story of how the film was made. I asked him what he thought the theme of the film was in contrast to what others may think. All he said about the theme was that it was about "coming home." By ten o'clock, I had plenty notes for my story and was now free to ask questions dear to me. For example, what was Garr doing when he was my age?

"How old are you?"

"Late twenties."

"Back then I was back and forth between Colorado and LA working for an independent film producer, story editing. Gradually moved up in the ranks from third unit director stuff to some DP work. Eventually a friend and I started a production shingle with money from his rich family. One of our first films grossed ten million. The way we structured the distribution, I never had to work again." Garr said the key was from then on to live simply and make films on his terms using other people's money.

"So simple," I said.

"Easier said than done but since I am now an old man, I can look back with hindsight and say this was exactly how I intended my life to work out."

"Bullshit," I countered, to him laughing heartily. I wanted to know more. Did he have a wife? Children?

"Married at twenty-two, had two sons. Divorced four years later. Cohabitation never my thing. My sons started a brothers money managing business and I recommended all my rich Hollywood friends to give their money to them."

"How could they be so different?"

"Managing money requires an untold amount of creativity. You wouldn't believe some of the IRS loopholes with overseas incorporation, non-profits and so on."

"Was creativity in whatever shape or form the essence of life?"

"Fuck if I know."

I left his house with a freezer bag of Serrano peppers and drove half drunk down the two track back to my house. I arrived around one in the morning and typed up my notes as soon as I got to my laptop. I didn't want to let anything slip through the cracks of my own feeble, inebriated memory. I knew I had a good story for the column and extra material to pitch for one of Aspen's glossy magazines. A culinary story set in Harry Garr's kitchen perhaps, or maybe a story about his attitude toward his property and the parallels found in his films. I don't know, but there is plenty of material for me to twist into a story.

The real coup for me though was Garr's invitation to come back whenever I pleased, if I didn't mind helping out on the property. If there's one thing I am certain of, I know I will be back there soon. In the morning, I cooked eggs with spinach and Garr's peppers. The ones I ate the previous evening were tangy sweet. The big one I minced into my eggs was sent from hell.

Of course I was going to bring a lady with me to the Garr screening but which one, Lyons, Eve, or Alyssa? The risk was that I would run into one or both of the others that I didn't end up taking. My thought was Alyssa wouldn't be interested in going without an invitation from me, Eve would want to go and likely would go if I didn't invite her, but Lyons would be the one I would enjoy most spending the time with. Wasn't it yesterday Alyssa had a firm hold on my heart? Lyons would be the most difficult to pin down. Why is it that what is harder to come by is also more desirous? Maybe that's just me.

I called her after lunch, didn't bother texting, and got her voice mail. I felt an unnatural amount of disappointment that she didn't pick up the phone. And when she called back later that afternoon, my heart fluttered. I asked if she would like to join me to the movie the following evening. She accepted and invited me to her place for drinks beforehand. For the rest of the day and night and subsequent morning I was in a Lyons trance thinking of nothing except her. By noon I was able to detach myself from my own thinking and wonder what had come over me. The great deal of respect I now had toward Garr saved me and I was able to focus on my work as journalist for the evening ahead.

* * *

Lyons poured us red wine and I sat on a tall stool talking to her as she moved around her apartment putting on her evening outfit, texting her friends, gathering herself. Our conversation ranged from the principles of our love making, and what it meant to each of us, to the troubles she was having with her mother. I wanted to talk more about our intimacy because it became clear to me that we had a different approach to it. Regarding her mother, I could only offer to be patient and endure. I said I thought sex was an expression of love, and she didn't disagree. Where we differed was that she thought it was the penultimate goal post for validating a courtship. She said she had carnal experience with men who would then leave and never talk to her again. I said that was crude behaviour befit for a man totally unlike myself. She was skeptical. Men are by nature inconsiderate, thinking of themselves as the only dog on the block, despite the presence of others.

I checked my watch and noticed we were late. We rushed out the door toward the Wheeler. When we arrived, the only seats left were in the back. I wasn't sure, nor was anyone including the event organizers (so I was told later) whether Garr would come up on stage afterward to answer questions from the audience. When the film ended, there was a healthy volume of clapping. Everyone stayed to watch the credits. Was everyone clapping out of respect or because they were genuinely entertained by the film? I don't know and I didn't bother wasting time on such a question that my younger self would have dwelled on to distraction. Lyons said she liked the film a lot. I thought it wasn't all that engrossing and lacked pace and wit. But I did respect the man to a great degree and tried to see the film for what it was. Garr never made it on stage and since I was "media," I was allowed backstage with Lyons.

There, I saw Garr in conversation with a constant stream of people. Alyssa was there taking photos. She saw me with Lyons and shook her head. Nothing more. With Garr, an opening for me to say hello and introduce Lyons never came. But he did smile over to me and wave and that was more than enough. Maybe I would go back to visit him next week. That would be more genuine anyway. Lyons and I returned to her apartment and we soon were sharing her bed. She once again refused to make love with me, saying she needed more proof that I wouldn't run off after.

* * *

I woke with a headache. It was half past six and upon rolling out of bed, all

Lyons could offer was a grunt. She would be out for another three hours I suspected. That kind of blissful sleep-in was out of the question for me. Looking out the east window of Lyon's kitchen, all I could see was grey overcast. Weather to match my mental state. Hunger drove me to snoop the kitchen and in it I found nothing except old broccoli. How could she live like this? There needs to be at least a loaf of bread in the kitchen of wherever I live, along with coffee. All the time. I took a hot shower in the bathroom next to where Lyons was dead asleep. Would she wake and get food with me? I felt dreary on a hungover Saturday morning without sunshine, food, and companionship. I also had work to do in writing up how the screening went. I have my own questions about writing still unanswered. Is it best served when I am feeling above all in good spirits? Or is it nothing more than how a nail appears to a carpenter waiting to be hammered. Somewhere in between is how I always conclude such a maddening thought.

This morning, the prospect of writing about last night was to be nothing more than banging nails in wood. This thought troubled me because there was an associated feeling gnawing at me that I was short-changing my work and subject matter. I cared about both, tremendously. Coffee, eggs and bread were my last hope and I left a gently snoring Lyons a note on her kitchen table telling her to come look for me at our favourite cafe in town if she woke in the next hour and otherwise to please do her guests a favour by stocking provisions other than old broccoli.

I walked straight past a bus stop on my way into town thinking a walk would do me well before breakfast. Perhaps walking and calories would lift me from my deadened mood. I was pleased at the notion that such simple medicine may do the job. I was thinking Alyssa wouldn't want to see me outside of work anymore. With Lyons, our favourite cafe didn't yet exist because we had yet to spend time in one together. Nor had we ever even spoken of one. But I thought writing that on a note would make her feel a warmth upon her reading it when she woke. However trivial, I thought it was proposition without risk that she would try finding me. Town was quiet but it was still off-season and not yet eight in the morning. My truck was parked at Buttermilk so as to avoid me paying for parking. I didn't know where to go for my much anticipated breakfast and so ducked into the first attractive cafe. A cute little place in an old house with a historical plaque posted near the entrance.

I sat down with a cappuccino to read the Herald while waiting for my scrambled eggs and toast. The front page had a story about politics which I ignored flipping through to look for a juicy column. I did a spit take when I saw a column published from the evasive Carlyle Erikson. I had given up trying to speak with him for my story after his repeated blowing me off. The column was his resignation letter from the Roaring Fork Institute. I won't go into the details of what he said only that he was doing so in the "best interests of the organization." His new title? President of Westcott Foundation's Indian Economic Development Fund. His new office location? Taos, New Mexico.

After my breakfast which did make me feel considerably better, I phoned mom to ask if she'd heard of what Erikson was up to in Taos. Even in town, I had trouble picking up a reliable signal. An annoyance and surprise given Aspen's degree of wealth, but also a kind of throwback to when we weren't so tethered to our phones. Mom said she'd heard a few days ago about Erikson from one of her clients. All that was known in Taos was that Erikson was going to be announced soon as the new head of an organization focused on channeling funds from this country's major philanthropies toward various causes, all related to the well-being of Native Americans. I asked mom to keep me up to date because I knew she would be learning more given her stature in Taos' social strata. I told her that he was implicated, or so I had come to believe, in an illegal cigarette distribution business across the southwest. Mom laughed deeply when she heard my accusation, but after I told her more about my findings, she said before hanging up "Never a dull day with you."

In the Pitkin County jail there was a South Korean oil and cigarette heir with strong ties to Erikson. In Taos, Erikson was about to be named to a prominent Native American development agency. In Aspen there were a few different characters including the sheriff, all at least somewhat in the know of cheap cigarettes flooding the market. How much of this should I report back to Norman? I was thinking he wouldn't give two shits unless there was actually something to report on for his paper. Perhaps this story really would turn the heads of our national newspapers or magazines. A dream of mine ever since reading as a high schooler Lewis' reporting on the European financial mess. I've been wary of Greek bonds ever since.

I walked from the cafe to the Rubey Transit Centre to wait for a bus to Buttermilk. That's where I saw Lyons storming toward me. I smiled at her, sensing I was in for trouble. "Good Morning," I said. She scowled. She didn't like having to walk around town guessing where I was. She apparently had been in every single cafe in town and then saw my "sorry ass" walking toward the bus stop. I told her I didn't think she'd be up for breakfast in time. The whole ordeal resulted in her saying she needed to take a break from me on account of not wanting to be left "on an island." We argued some, and then my bus arrived. She said she needed space. I could't believe the turn our relationship had just taken.

On the down valley bus, I received a lengthy text message from her. She said she wasn't sure if I was committed to her so why should she be toward me. The emotional vagaries of this woman were complex and unpredictable. My first instinct would be to reply with a couple of words and let the storm pass over. But I was upset that she was treating me this way and so I took the time to write out an even longer message than the one she sent me to explain my side of what happened. And to go over the past week's events to explain why I was in fact committed to her and ready for even deeper commitment. Her reply to mine was short and missed all the points that I brought up. She said she was leaving to Denver the next day to stay with a friend. She would be back later next week.

All I could think to say to her was "Safe travel." I got off the bus and there was my truck. I drove to the horse farm. I needed to focus on writing the story about Garr's premiere. Strangely, I felt in a perfect mental place to write. The kind of feeling that keeps me in this business because it sure isn't something I do for the money. Hell, dinner and breakfast last night ate up my future earnings for this very story. But then when I think about it, it's kind of a beautiful thing where my writing pays for the necessities of life. It's a clean way to move through the world. An even trade.

I finished the story after sweating it out for a few hours playing with different ways to start the thing. Garr's picture was about an iconoclastic young woman bent on traveling from Los Angeles to San Francisco, to dump her drug dealing hippie boyfriend. I thought it was a clever take on two seemingly connected movements, that of free love and woman's rights, butting against each other. How two idealistic characters with differing views on what it means to live by trial and fire can't come to terms with their own relationship. In writing and directing the film, perhaps there was material mined from Garr's own life. Hemingway said of writing, to start with what you know and go elsewhere. I like to think of that approach as a stable point of departure.

In any event, I called Norman around five in the evening to tell him that I had the story ready and would send it later that night. I was done and could've sent it then, but I needed to let the thing marinate. Would Garr read what I'd written? I was quoting him, including some racy stories of how the picture was made. At the very least I did not want to disappoint him with what I'd come up with. Norman asked if I'd managed any photos, to which I said no. I was unaware I needed any. He said back to me before hanging up: "Aren't you a journalist?"

Without internet at my place, I couldn't email the producers of the event, so I had to get in my truck and drive to the nearest place with signal. In Carbondale, I pulled over on the side of the street and emailed the people at the Wheeler. They replied surprisingly within a few minutes with a Google Drive link to a series of photos. I forwarded the link to Norman and he got back to me asking for a shot of Garr in his house. Adding, "weren't you just there?" I was, but now I had to go back. Whether Garr would let me take one was another matter. All I could do was try and so off I went as the sun dipped below the mountain. At a liquor store, I bought a bottle of expensive Tequila and in no time I was walking up Garr's front porch. From outside, I could hear latin jazz and people laughing. Garr was having a get together. I felt nervous for arriving unannounced. But the man did say to come by anytime. Here I was.

I knocked hard on the door and there an off-duty Bledsoe greeted me. The Pitkin County sheriff was holding a full glass of red wine, his face flushed. A joint dangled between his fingers. He welcomed and recognized me right away. I put the bottle of tequila on the table and asked about Garr. Bledsoe said he was out back with a girlfriend. I asked who else was here, and Bledsoe replied, just a few "other homeys." I didn't know much about Bledsoe, only that he was perhaps as much a hippie as Garr. I remember Norman telling me he was deputy sheriff down in Garfield County for close to twenty years, the whole time chafing under a hard right winger. When the opportunity for Pitkin County sheriff came up, his reputation for being lenient got him easily elected. So of course I found him here, inebriated among friends in Harry Garr's house.

Where was Garr? Not long after I arrived and I finished my first vin rouge, did he come wheeling around the corner from a hallway leading to his bedroom. In tow was a strikingly beautiful woman of around my age. I recognized her. Garr greeted me like I was an old friend and poured me another full glass. "You're staying here tonight, buster, Heather, your friends arriving?" It was Heather from Halloween night with Alyssa. She said yes, they were on their way. I felt a warm glow envelop me. The night was going in an unplanned direction. But would Alyssa even speak to me after the premiere? My Lyons blues had bummed me out and how come Eve hadn't reached out? I suppose Alyssa had good reason. Is it always up to the male to initiate a plan or conversation? I asked Garr if we could get a photo together. I gave my phone to Bledsoe and right before he took it I pretended to drop something to remove myself from the frame. The photo was one of Garr in fine form by a row of cacti in his living room. Perfect. I told him later after more booze and God knows what else, that I hoped to use it for my story. I needed to get it to Norman that night. Later on I sent it without Garr's permission. The thing was going in tomorrow's paper, that was for damn sure.

When Alyssa arrived as part of the Heather entourage, I was at first surprised. Those feelings quickly dissipated. Of course she would be here tonight at Harry Garr's. She was evidently among a group of girls in this valley that could be asked out by old rich guys one moment, ski bums working 1A the next. Broad sex appeal to any subset of man. Alyssa spotted me while I was mid conversation with Bledsoe's girlfriend, the owner of Tony's (an old Aspen eatery). She walked by saying just loud enough for only me to hear: "a little old for you don't you think?" Bledsoe's girlfriend by then having directed her attention to her boyfriend. I got up and walked toward this enigma of a woman and poured some of my tequila in her glass. Tequila, she said, her strongest aphrodisiac. That gave my worm a good turn and I blushed.

She laughed, slugged the drink and grabbed me by the hand leading me to a bedroom. I remember thinking that this couldn't actually be happening. But it was and it did. We made love in Garr's master bedroom. After, she slapped me hard on the face. She said, "I don't want you seeing anyone else, okay hun?"

"Promise," I said.

"I'm good at revenge."

Garr's was Falstaffian. We drank gallons and ate pounds of fine wine and food. Conversation ranged from Chinese poetry to Colorado water rights. I was out of my depth, but I tried to keep pace as if running a sub three hour marathon. Alyssa, Heather and the girls stayed until four in the morning and were picked up by a shadowy figure in an SUV. When the girls left, it was Garr, myself, and a couple of others. Bledsoe and his girl had long gone to bed. It was just as the dust started to settle from the vehicle peeling out of the driveway when Garr suggested we go "hunt some bird." I looked at him like he was mad, but how could I say no? The dogs were baying out the back door at something and Garr said the predawn light was a perfect time for us to start our outward trek to find us some bird. So that's what we did. The others stayed back for sleep. I borrowed some of Garr's hunting gear and off we walked from the north edge of his property in a direction toward bird.

"What're we hunting?"

"Columbian Sharp-Tailed Grouse. You get me drinkin' like this, I gotta kill or shoot somethin'."

I followed, shotgun in hand, through thick sagebrush as the atmosphere slowly brightened. We didn't say a word to one another. We were made silent by our thoughts. The dogs breathed hard, racing around wild. We walked for a few miles before the sun came blazing over mountains to the east. Finally we arrived to where he wanted to start the hunt. Garr called in the dogs and then presented them a feather for scent. The dogs began a sniffing campaign as Garr and I gingerly walked through gently rolling fields. There was a cold north wind. My hands holding the gun had long gone numb without gloves. I took a long pull from a canteen of water, lost in thought and... BANG!

Garr pulled his trigger. Never before had I shot a gun. I made sure to not tell Garr. Off the dogs ran toward the fallen bird. Garr's shot succeeded. One of the dogs brought back the dead bird and with that, Garr said we were done. We now had our breakfast. We returned to the house taking a different, more scenic route. Garr was much more talkative on our return. I was trying to understand how this octogenarian had the kind of stamina to do what we just did after the night we just went through. I felt like shit on the walk back.

We got back at nine. I put coffee on while Garr cleaned the bird. "I'm gon' fry this sombitch with eggs n' bacon," he said. The turn-around time was astonishing for us to be eating a bird that only a few hours earlier was alive and well flying through the Colorado air on a crisp November morning. The moody clouds from yesterday were nonexistent. Over grouse, eggs and bacon, Garr and I drank coffee in his airy, sunlit kitchen. The others slept through the entire episode. Morning birds sang. When Garr asked me near the end of our meal how far I was willing to go nosing around the "Syndicate," I almost choked on my grouse.

I told him I would take it as far as it needed to be taken. The "ordeal" was apparently a touchy subject for Garr because I could see that he was wrestling over how to respond to my response. I asked him if he had a stake in the business. Or whether his sons had invested his money in the racket to take advantage of some arcane tax loophole. Garr said nothing. All he would say to me afterward and before asking me to be on my way was that I be careful not to "ruffle too many feathers." The money from that operation helped sustain a lifestyle that needn't be disrupted. I thought it was a poor way to end the evening, night, and morning. But I wasn't going to apologize for doing my job. I am a journalist and as one paper I used to work for said as their motto: "If you don't want it printed, don't let it happen." Garr threw another curveball by suggesting as I got up to leave that Alyssa was someone to be even more careful around. I thought this was rather silly, thinking he was nothing more than a jealous old guy. I said thanks, and left. Was Garr on my side? I drove the two-track toward Carbondale in need of heavy rest. Enough of this hedonistic living.

* * *

By midweek I was back to the grind and thinking nothing of the weekend escapade at Garr's. The whole thing made my head spin. I was busy on the phone doing interviews for various stories. I had to think of my next column. Norman was asking more questions about the Chung piece. Each day he would ask me if I'd gotten any further on interviewing people like Chung, his lawyer, the sheriff, etc. I eventually had to tell him I had things under control and to stop micromanaging. I think his pride was hurt with my tone and vigor. Finally he took me out for a coffee and apologized. He missed being a reporter in the "trenches."

"What about the Arapaho lead? Any word?"

"No. And I tried calling the guy back who told me about him, my family friend."

"What he say?"

"He has a landline that goes unanswered."

"We need to talk to that guy. What's his name again?"

"Stan said Darwin. I know. So many other things going on right now."

"Well, why don't you let me try and track him down at least?"

"Yeah? You think you can do that?"

"Watch me." Two days later, Norman had a phone number for me to call. He sent me an email with the contact information for Darwin Hamilton of La Junta.

I asked, "How'd you do that?"

"Do what?"

"Track Darwin down so fast?"

"You're surprised?"

"Norman, come on. How the hell you do that?"

"Not bad for an old guy eh? When you are trying to find someone, you gotta think about who may know of someone who may know and so on. And just try and try some more. Darwin turns out, is still fairly visible and active about tribal affairs. Helps also he's on La Junta's town council."

"All right, I'll call him right away."

"You want, I could."

"Norm. Come on. This is mine."

"All right, all right. Thought I'd ask."

Darwin Hamilton and I spoke on the phone later that night. He asked how I'd heard of him. I mentioned Stan being a family friend, where I was from, and what I was working on. I could tell from his clipped voice and monosyllabic answers he wasn't willing to start gushing out any information. Darwin was guarded. I kept pestering him though to open up. Finally, after telling him about some of the other stories I'd published, he started talking.

"Meko," Darwin said, "You sure you want to go down this road?"

"Yeah, I'm sure."

"You say you're familiar with Dianne Westcott?"

"Met her the other day."

"How long you been in Aspen?"

"Since October."

"You plan on stayin'?"

"Why you ask?"

"Chasing this thing down, you may not be welcome there much longer all I'm sayin'."

"Oh yeah?"

"Yeah. Anyway, I got a binder full of documents you may find of interest when we tried to take Westcott to court. I'm drivin' through to Utah start of December, you want we could meet in Glenwood."

"Glenwood it is."

"And I'm not kiddin' about these people, Meko. You're sure?"

"I understand. Yeah, I'm sure."

"All right well if you change your mind..."

"Mr. Hamilton, Can't thank you enough."

"See you in Glenwood. We'll be in touch."

* * *

Ski season was still a couple weeks away and I needed money. There was three hundred sixty eight dollars in my bank account. I started to think about ways to make a buck. December rent was around the corner. I also had the contact from Yasiel to rake leaves before the first snow. I would do that for a few hundred, no problem. Knowing I could rake leaves left me feeling much better. I called Yasiel's uncle Don, and the plan was soon set. I would rake leaves from eight in the morning until one in the afternoon for ten straight days. Don agreed to pick me up at the Brush Creek intercept lot each morning. This was irrigation all over again.

I told Norman what I was doing. He thought it was a good idea and wondered if he could pick up on the Chung piece where I had left off. No, I told him. Chung piece was mine. Though I was sick of dealing with the story with its dead ends, I told him I needed a break from it. I was keen to lose myself in physical labour. The Herald's publisher also thought it was a good idea for me to take a break. She wanted to conserve her freelance budget for when things got cranking over ski season.

* * *

Wasn't it yesterday I arrived to find entire mountainsides yellow from changing leaves? It was now my job to rake up those very leaves. I was picked up by Don in an old truck at half past seven on a Thursday morning, ready to rake. By midmorning, I had blisters on both hands and a sore back. House after house, we raked leaves. I had the rake, Don had the blower. He was working seven days a week, ten hour days to bank hours and cross off as many houses as possible from the list given to him by his boss. Whenever in the truck driving from one house to another, Don would put on the weather station. He wanted to know if there was snow on the way. I asked him what he was going to do once raking was over. His plan was to return to work as a waiter at a mid mountain restaurant on Highlands. Big tips. Don later told me a large portion of his income goes to his family who lives in Texas on the border. Outskirts of El Paso. I asked him why he came to work in Aspen. Skiing, girls, parties, money. Before or after he was married? Before, he said. He married a housekeeper from the St. Regis who still lives in the valley.

After raking leaves, I would either bus down valley to the intercept lot to retrieve my truck, or stay in town and visit the library. All of the houses we raked were in Aspen. I used my free time at the library to get busy with my novel. I didn't know what I was doing, but I just kept writing. My goal was to do two thousand words per day. And the novel's length needed to be greater than sixty thousand words. I was writing a western. I had always wanted to write one and thought the hell with it, let me try writing genre. I didn't want it to be like Portis, Wister, Grey, or anyone. If anything I wanted it to be fresh like how Goldman wrote Butch Cassidy.

My setting was Colorado and the era was the late nineteenth century. There, it was a western no matter the plot. The plot was about a guy just like me moving to a small Colorado town to work as a journalist. Twain once was a journalist, what if there was a Twainian type character living in a Colorado mining town writing a journal? That was the MO for my story. Life as a journalist in Old Colorado. The "fresh" aspect to the writing would be my voice. It would sing on the page or it wouldn't. There would be observations on wildlife, money, women and hardship. There was my novel. In the library, I looked up old newspaper archives from Herald stories published way back to use as inspiration for my own story. My character was writing about current events and what did I know of what was going on back then.

* * *

After three days of raking, I heard from the Coutinho's. Gabriel asked me of my availability and credentials. I replied saying I was a former NCAA Division 1 ski racer with coaching and instructing experience at all levels. I had the bare bones minimum coaching certificate required to work and be insured. No way would I ever think to go all the way and receive my level three or four from whatever governing body assigned such credentials. I laugh when ski instructors who can barely arc a turn prance around bars telling everyone of their credentials.

Gabriel was impressed with my background and asked if I would be willing to teach his two girls how to race. Eve would still have Gabriel, and I would take care of his daughters. I quoted him a price for half day and full day lessons. Since this arrangement was to be outside of the official Aspen Mountain Ski School, my idea was to quote a price just under their top rate. Eve had told me top instructors charged a thousand bucks before tips for a full day on Ajax. I mentioned that figure in a previous missive. It still astonishes me. I was also licking my lips.

I quoted Gabriel nine hundred for a full day per kid and five hundred for a half day. There would be days, he said, where he would also like my instruction. I asked for how long they would be in Aspen, and like he said when we first started emailing, three or four weeks. From the second week of December through to the first week of January, I would be skiing everyday with his two daughters. He asked if I wanted to do a contract or if I was a "handshake guy." I said the latter. The amount of money I'd be making made me think: only in Aspen. How the rich can spend.

Once the deal with Gabriel was finalized I thought to myself, what am I doing raking leaves at fifteen bucks an hour for the next six days? But I had made an agreement to Don and I would hold up my end of the bargain. The physical labour of raking leaves, as menial as it was, I think made my writing better. Physicality calms me and opens up my creative channels. What I would end up doing with my novel, I had no clue. I suppose I would just send it cold to literary agents and book publishers. Such small odds for success, but can't know unless I try. What was my marker for success? That I was happy with it? That a publisher agreed to print copies of it? I had to wrestle with the meaning of why I was doing this. At least I enjoyed the writing.

When I was living in Oregon, a writer friend said that lots of agents like to see a collection of short stories as a point of departure. I am not opposed to writing short stories, I just like the idea right now of writing standalone novels. A novelist. Writing broad appeal, grocery store paperback type stories. Nice way to make a buck.

* * *

I found out Don was friends with Pete Christopher my fifth day raking leaves. From way back. Naturally I asked if he was aware of the Syndicate. Don said, of course. I was shocked he was so frank with me. Perhaps because he was unaware of me being a journalist. Don said it was a "nice little business for those guys." I asked him who those guys were, expecting the same names I was aware of. He said he wasn't entirely sure but he knew the sheriff and a couple of his friends somehow were involved and also some "bigwigs." With Don, I was uncertain if I should broach the subject of his past involvement with the Sinaloa. Or whether he was aware of any connection the cartel may have with the Syndicate. In the end, I asked him point blank. All he said was his involvement was from a prior chapter of his life. He would not elaborate any further. I never asked him again. I told him I heard that the South Korean guy arrested was involved and also the guy who used to run the

sult of my effort. I was Van Morrison cleaning windows, reading Christmas Humphreys' book on Zen. Don was good company.

On the car ride back to my truck at the end of the day I took a risk by bringing up my troubles with Lyons. I didn't expect much of anything from him, but hell, aren't women something most guys can relate back to? God knows what constituted Don's attitude toward women. I was interested. When I told him about Lyons' out of the blue decision to call our relationship quits, Don wanted to know more. I told him the story in as succinct a way as possible. Country music was on the radio instead of Don's typical weather reports. "Cowboys like smoky old poolrooms and clear mountain mornings." Don turned it louder and lit a joint. Don wanted to remove any barriers to our conversation about women. I don't smoke but I felt obliged to do so upon his offering. And, well, it worked. We had a good honest chat and when he dropped me off at my truck, I sure felt better about the whole thing. It was one of those feelings of having something heavy lifted off your back that you didn't even know was there in the first place.

Don's take was that women on occasion need space. Need time to think, find their own clarity. Whatever Lyons' reasoning was for our break, she may have a perfectly logical argument in her own mind. Whether she was good at articulating it, another matter. So was my own biased take on how our relationship had been progressing. Don said hindsight is hard to trust for truth and accuracy. That's why we communicate, was my thinking, so that these kinds of problems can be addressed, worked out. Don said maybe I had been missing signals all along about where and what to communicate about. It's an insecure thing to mull, and I think that's where regret is birthed. I felt regret for not being better with Lyons. Don said, better how? Just better. Don began telling me about problems with his wife. It was funny, the things that tangled him up, I saw as simple problems easily resolved. We are in our own petri-dish and so how can we examine objectively our own behaviour? My problems, Don's problems, I guess that's why they are called problems.

I recall one of my undergraduate mathematics professors saying when I visited (often) his office hours that the problems he was giving us were easy. Solutions to all of them were known. For math PhD's, they have to live with unsolved problems for entire lifetimes. Often never finding a solution. How does one grapple with a problem unsolved? Is this where mental heuristics and biases get us in trouble? My problem with Lyons, to solve it perhaps there was a different approach required. Out of the box thinking, that kind of mumbo jumbo. What should I do? How should I do? My default wasn't working. Must be a better way. A way that resonates with her. Her being Lyons, the one and only.

* * *

Charlie Munger likes to say when trying to solve a difficult problem, "inverse, always inverse." Something like that. Anyway, how could I inverse my approach to Lyons? As I fed oats to June, an inverse occurred to me. If my default was to ask to see her, to talk to her, what would the inverse be? Let her go in my mind. Cease communication. But what if she were to take my silence as evidence that we were in fact done? That I had moved on? It was a risk. But hell, what were my options. Inverse, always inverse.

June was shivering in the cold evening air. There was a gust from the east and I too started shivering. I wanted to ride June and so resolved to ask Donna if this was a possibility. How fun, the prospect of riding June through the Elk Mountains that are my backyard. On a clear mountain morning. The evening light was fading fast on account of the cloud cover and it wasn't long before I bid my friend goodnight. I couldn't get "inverse, always inverse" out of my head as I lay in bed. It's really an optimistic way to move through life, the idea that yes problems are solvable with a flexible mind. I slept deeply that night and woke to a clear mountain morning in late November. Aspen's leaves needed raking and I was to help do that job.

* * *

Ajax opened yesterday. I was told it was one of the best season openers in thirty years. From the south a storm came charging up from the Pacific. It was cold enough in the Elk Mountains to produce a foot of snow. The storm also meant I was done raking leaves. I didn't ski yesterday because although we had a tremendous amount of snow on the valley floor, there was still work to be done closing up the landscaping business for the winter. The rocky base of the mountain probably still bare on parts of what was open to the public. Don and I were hauling equipment up and down the valley to get it all into storage. The boss was down in Baja relaxing before a busy season skiing and working his other job managing a ski shop.

The proximity of Ajax to town meant that as we worked through the course of the day, I could peer to the south side of the valley and see skiers slide their way down the mountain. I had a yearning to ski, unlike any I had felt in a long time. I wanted wind in the face, as an old ski racing friend used to say. Wind in the face. Don and I were in a sort of festive mood. He of course would be going straight to work without a break at his other job. I was wondering what a waiter needed to do before a restaurant opened. "Lots," he said. He helped operate the cat with another guy that drove the food, booze and such up the mountain each day. The restaurant had yet to be stocked for its opening. Don asked if I had given any more thought to my situation with Lyons and I said that I was going to try something different and cease communication. He winced at the idea but recognized it as just another tactic. He nodded.

We changed subjects to skiing. He asked me if I was going to be doing much of it this year. I told him I hoped to do lots in the backcountry. Don didn't know what that meant, so I explained to him the notion of skiing without chairlifts, ski passes, mid-mountain restaurants and so on. He couldn't understand why anyone would want to hike up a mountain before sliding down. I told him that if he were to have spent the amount of time on skis like me, from age two onward, and for the most part going around gates, getting out in the backcountry was essential. For the soul. How skiing was once done before mechanical chairlifts. Free the heel, free the mind. The important thing, wind in the face. He liked that. He said he could use some of that too about now. It was lunchtime on a Sunday.

In the early twilight of that November afternoon, Don dropped me off at my truck. Our work day was complete. I was doubtful I would see Don again. We said we would try and go for a ski, or that I would stop by his restaurant, but I think he and I knew that if we were to see each other again, it would be raking leaves in the spring. I was confident that I would not be raking come spring given my income projections working with Gabriel's family. I live cheap. Don drove away and I watched as he did until he was out of sight.

I got in my truck, fired it up and drove into town to drop my skis off at a shop for a tuning and to pick up my season pass. Eve had finagled me a pass as an "associate instructor" and instructed me to mention her name at a ski shop in town for a few free ski tunings. My skis, the ones I used all the time no matter the terrain, were designed for the backcountry. I had pin bindings on them which are light and meant for the heel piece to turn on an axis to free the heel. And my boots, old things that came with the skis and bindings I purchased used from a mountain guide two years ago. Couple hundred bucks I paid for equipment that new costs over two grand. The edges on my skis needed sharpening.

For the past few ski seasons, I was doing nothing really except going into the backcountry of wherever I was living. Montana, New Mexico, I even did a trip up into the interior of British Columbia, God's skiing country. Again, no lifts for me. Only the wild side of skiing. Getting a season pass for the season and having my skis go in for tuning, altogether reminiscent of a time for me long gone. Not since my days skiing at Dartmouth had I started a ski season off like this.

I found the shop at the base of Ajax that Eve told me to go to. I walked in around five in the evening wearing dirty Carhartts, an insulated plaid work jacket and a ball cap. I looked working class and this ski shop was unlike any I had ever set foot in. It was a Euro-chic big money kind of place. There was a cafe, the walls were lined with new ski boots, goggles, gloves, there were animal skin throws draped over the chairs. Tucked far back in the store was the division for boot fittings and ski tunings.

A babe was there to greet me. She looked at me, the outfit I was in, and presumed I was lost. I told her a friend of mine, Eve, told me to come here. At the mention of Eve's name, the girl lit right up and introduced herself. Monica. Turns out, Monica and Eve used to instruct together on Buttermilk before Monica decided she would rather work out of the cold and before Eve received the credentials to instruct on Ajax.

She said, "Anyone a friend of Eve's is a friend here. What can I do for you?"

"These skis need to be sharpened and waxed. And there's a core shot here..."

"Hand 'em over."

"Thanks. Can I pick them up tomorrow?"

"First thing." I thanked her again.

"You don't look familiar. This your first season?"

"Yeah, I only just moved here this fall from Taos."

"What brought you here?"

"A job. I work for the Herald, Do some instructing too."

"Well, welcome," she beamed. "How'd you meet Eve?"

"Dating app." Monica laughed, as I thought she would. People can be shy about admitting to others where they met a romantic interest. I didn't care.

"So you're the one."

"She's mentioned me?"

"Of course, we're like best friends."

I left my skis there and told Monica I needed to get my pass before the office next door closed. I walked over to find a line out the front door, but one that I didn't mind waiting in. Eventually I got my ski pass and the moment the woman behind the counter gave it to me, I once again felt an irrepressible urge to go skiing. Tomorrow, first chair. Off-season was over.

* * *

Norman sent an email that night saying my services wouldn't be needed until a few days into December. I had a week off in front of me, marginal pre-season ski conditions, a novel to work on, and a meeting with Darwin Hamilton around the corner. My bank account would soon swell by many percentage points after depositing the check Don had given me. Five hundred and eighty six bucks would bring my net worth close to a grand. December rent would be taken care of with ease. I had three weeks before Gabriel's arrival. That meant that in those three weeks, no matter what would happen in the international legal system regarding Chung, I could write the best story possible about his situation and the Syndicate. There was a time I felt like I was onto something with this story. But now I feel like no matter how damning it turns out to be, the story won't do much to disturb the Aspen peace. I hope I'm wrong.

* * *

I was riding up the Bell Mountain chair the next morning unaware of how lucky I was. Bell, or lift 5, is one of those old two-seater's most ski resorts in Aspen's category have long gone away with. Too slow, uncomfortable for the modern skier. Not me. I rode the thing all day since the skiing in its vicinity was really the only terrain open at this early date. The decision was made to open the lift since the mountain managers had not planned for the top of Ajax to be ready so soon. In any case, the chair was open and after this week, wouldn't reopen until April. Too much money to run the thing once the Gondola started spinning. The visibility was low, the skiing was marginal, but there was that wind in the face. First chair to last, I skied. By end of day, Spar Gulch (Aspen's central run) was a skating rink. Enough for me. I skied to the bottom and went in for a beer at the ski shop.

Monica was there, she asked about the skiing. Great, I said. I ordered a European beer I'd never heard of and sat watching the exotic scene of this most unusually high end ski shop. Eve came in through the doors with what looked like clients. She embraced Monica before she saw me and came over to say hello. Her clients were at the cafe's counter ordering booze.

"I saw you out there today, but I don't think you saw me." All the instructors looked the same to me with their bright red and silver uniforms.

"Sorry, was zoned in."

"Not bad up there right?"

"No, great for November."

"Another storm coming in a couple days."

"Met your friend Monica. She's great. You're great. Thanks for setting me up."

Eve winked. "Skiers look after one another. You're a skier."

"How can I return the favour?"

"How about rescuing me from these people?"

"How do I do that?"

"Just come join, and then I'll say we have to go to an event since you're a journalist." I joined Eve and sat with her and her clients. An older couple, in their early seventies. Ted and May Gaffney, from Dallas. A big time lawyer Eve told me later. I said I knew. That we'd met some time ago. Ted didn't remember me. To be expected.

I was bored to tears until Ted mentioned Chung. I bolted upright in my chair and took a deep gulp from my Euro beer. Tasted like fruit juice. I said I was working on a story about Chung for one of the paper's here in town. Ted said he knew the guy's lawyer. I cut him off. "You know Ari?" Ted said he did. I'd forgotten this. Ted knew Ari. That he wished him well. He didn't elaborate but I knew he was referring to Ari's failing marriage. Eve interjected saying she had go the restroom. In her absence I asked Ted pointed questions. I was sure that as soon as Eve returned she would pull on my arm to leave. Ted was surprisingly frank and in the few minutes Eve was gone informed me that he could help "fill out the picture."

The upshot was that Ari was not handling his marriage and art issues well and had asked Ted to help with the case. I figured. Ted said he was much more forthcoming with "media types" and even offered to meet this week for a ski. How about tomorrow, I asked. He agreed to meet at the base at ten in the morning. I left charged up to celebrate this breakthrough and took Eve for Italian. We still had our ski pants on, and our skis leaned against the restaurant's exterior.

At the table, Eve asked me what I was working on. I told her the story. Not all the minor details per se, but the points of the story that would form the backbone to what I would eventually write for print. I told her about the innocuous break-in, how it led to meetings and interviews with the perpetrator and his lawyer. I told about the various people I'd met in the community who all seemed to know about the racket. And of course of the people I'd met who were involved. I told her about Erikson's surprising departure from the Roaring Fork Institute. I told her about the crazy coincidence running into Ted.

My monologue lasted until our bruschetta arrived. She of course didn't realize until I told her how fortuitous it was running into Ted. I didn't want to use our time together for me to talk about work, so I leapt at any opportunity to change the subject. I tried to talk skiing, but she wanted to know more about the Chung piece. Her client's client was in a way my client. Aspen's small. I relented and kept the conversation going, channeling it back to how her day of skiing was with Ted and May. She said it was boring, but at least she was skiing. I was curious how she ended up with them as clients. Eve said that she used to instruct Ted's brother from New York. By chance one day a few years back she was assigned to the brother and over the years came to know and work with Ted. Eve said that he was the odd kind of lawyer that stood for the rights of the kind of people arrested for taking and dealing drugs. Somehow he made a fortune doing so, while keeping one foot in the world of being cool, independent, brash. Minus the fortune, her description of Ted made me think George Hanson, *Easy Rider*.

By the time our entree's arrived we were on our second bottle. By now, I had learned that even Eve was aware of the Syndicate. She let it slip. Nothing of what I'd said to her was news. She said she even helped occasionally with distribution.

"With distribution! How?"

"Very minor, but there have been times where I needed a little extra to pay for life in Aspen in the off-season and drove someone's truck from A to B. That's all." This was a showstopper. Would she be willing to go on record? This would give my story so much more dimension. It would show how the tentacles of this thing spread throughout the community to help pay for the working person's living. And I could really dive into how a part of the enterprise worked.

"Absolutely not."

"Oh come on, won't you?"

"I know where this is going. I am going to stop you right now, or I will leave. I am not going on record for your little story. You know Meko, you can be so self-centred!"

Our food arrived and I was happy to just sit there and eat. I stopped pressing. Across from Eve who looked wonderful. I asked her if I could stay the night at hers. There was lots to keep me here. Not driving home, and being in town for tomorrow's ski with Ted.

"Come and go as you please."

"That's not what I meant."

I paid the bill, we grabbed our skis and walked back to her place. We made love until two in the morning.

Eve was up before me. She had clients to ski with, first chair. I got out of bed as she got on the lift. I had an hour before meeting Ted. What would I ask him? I didn't want to overthink this whole thing. If he opened up, great. I had decided that I was going to attribute what Eve told me last night to an anonymous source. Too rich to not.

At the base, I found Ted wearing an Austrian Eisbar hat. His ski suit was blue and white Bogner and he was holding a pair of red Atomic giant slalom race skis. It was going to be a day of groomers. Here I was with my equipment best suited to walking up and then skiing down through face shots of powder. He looked at me and shook his head, smiling. A real ski bum, he was thinking. I looked at him and thought this guy can either ski great or not at all. No in between. Given his Texas residence and time consuming occupation, I assumed the latter. I didn't care. We got on the Gondola spinning for the first time all season.

"That thing was how I met May thirty years ago," he said looking down at Bell from our gondola cabin.

"Which one? 5?"

"You know the numbers? Anyway, end of my second season here, I ski up to the chair after hot doggin' down Face of Bell and there she is about to get on solo. I pretend like I happen to just slide innocently in beside her just before we ski to the loading line and poof, this will be our thirty first wedding anniversary in a couple weeks. You sleepin' with Eve? How about Lyons?" Both questions, abrupt and startling. And he remembered Lyons!

"Am I what?"

"They're like daughters to me you know. May and I, we never had kids."

I cleared my throat.

"Nevermind. Forget I asked. Treat 'em right. That's all I need to tell you."

"Of course."

"You know, for a winter, spring and fall the second year we were dating, May wouldn't talk to me."

"Why is that?"

"Long story short, our relationship came to a point where she thought she hardly knew me. So I told her to ask me anything. First thing she asked, the only thing I might add, was whether I was seeing any other women in town. Back then I was wintering in Aspen, not giving one flying fuck about being a lawyer. Lucky I had my dad's firm to go back to and do grunt work for in Dallas when it wasn't ski season. Anyway, she asked, and I told her straight up that there had been others."

"And?"

"That's why she stopped talking to me."

"Yeah."

"This town, it's too small to do what I was doing. Still is that way. Keep your focus Meko."

"Yes, sir."

It was like I was momentarily under the spell of a father figure I never had. Shivers ran down my spine. I knew he was right, but here I was into several different burgeoning relationships, all with women I was naturally compelled toward.

"You seein' anyone else?"

"No sir. Course not."

"Good." We still had a good chunk of the ride left to the top of Ajax.

"Onto the next topic. Chung. What do you need to know?"

"More than just Chung at this point. I want to have my story expose what seems to me anyway common knowledge. I want it on paper."

"The cigarettes."

"Yes, and the enigmatic Syndicate behind it...whatever that is."

"I wouldn't go there."

"What everyone says."

"Let's put it this way, the upside, far as I can tell is that you the author may get recognition. Not just in town, but across the country. I were you, I would want the same. Maybe a big paper out east, they could hire you, am I right?"

"Of course."

"You're honest. But you know this will be a story that the paper lays claim on don't you? And the end result is that this little cash cow that helps prop up a handful of people's lives here, it gets taken down. And these people. Let me ask you something. You like living here?"

"Sure."

"You do this story, you won't want to live here anymore. You understand?"

"You're serious?"

"You think this is a joke?"

"This kind of story needs to be told. Last time I checked this isn't Moscow."

"Fuckin' right this ain't Moscow. But you gotta understand that this kind of attention will really only do you harm and it will harm those that you wish to write about." It was time now to get off the gondola. The wind was whipping from the west and the snow guns, they droned on. Pumping gallon after gallon of water turned to snow onto the mountain. We grabbed our skis from the exterior of our gondola cabin and walked toward a flat area to click in.

"All I'm saying kid is that the upside to you may appear like everything you want. But what I am telling you is that the reality is far from what you wish to happen. If you go ahead with the story."

"I hear what you are saying, and I'll take it in stride. Thank you."

All I could think to say was something cold, objective, emotionless. Something lawyerly. We skied down and then we kept skiing off lift 5. Ted was telling old stories of Aspen back in the day. About the ski gangs his buddies formed, about the old bars and saloons no longer around, about the hordes of Midwesterners that came out to live as ski bums.

It was a morning of skiing with an old Aspen dog. We skied down for lunch and Ted, on account of his knees, said he was done for the day. His skiing was mediocre. And of course he asked me for some tips after seeing how I was arcing my turns. I didn't need racing skis to carve, and Ted was astounded at how I was doing what I was doing. I told him to think about his pole plant and pressuring the outside ski at the top of the turn. At the bottom, and before we parted ways, he looked at me with a steely gaze.

"You're gonna do the story aren't you."

"Yup."

"Knew you would. But you gotta understand this ain't gonna be a fun place to live after you publish it."

"You decide yet if you wanna be an anonymous source? How long you in town for?"

"Week or so. Tomorrow night I'm taking May to a Thanksgiving dinner. Bring Eve along. After, we can all go back to my place up in Northstar and I'll give you some intel. Sound good?"

"Where for dinner?"

"Tony's. Seven thirty. Dress nicer than when I last saw you in street clothes."

"Yes sir."

Ted left toward the ski shop where May was waiting. I continued skiing until last lift. It was grey and cold and icy and it was still November.

Back at the horse farm that night, I read the day's Herald. There was nothing good in it save for a story they used from the Associated Press about wild horses in Colorado's Sand Wash Basin. In the north-west corner of the state, there was a wild horse with a coat pattern similar to that of a Picasso painting. Hence his name, Picasso. I was fascinated with the story of how those herds of wild horses could live off such hard scrabble land. It was a moving story and I couldn't help but think that this was the kind of journalism that I should be writing about. The natural world.

For me, crime wore thin. I didn't really care whodunit. It was just people doing things other people said illegal. That's the story. Nothing more. Wild horses in the American West. This is the kind of stuff people should be reading more about. I scissored the story out of the paper and kept it for my files. I told myself that after I was finished with the Chung piece, my new beat would be the environment. In my journalism and my fiction. Man's relationship with the natural world would be central in my novel about Old Colorado. Imagine, back then wolves were still around the Roaring Fork Valley. Not a chance now, even with efforts to reintroduce native wolf populations to this part of Colorado. The ranching lobby vetoed it on account of wolves being a threat to their pay dirt (herds of cattle). A disgusting notion that even locally, commerce trumps Mother Nature's will for her land.

* * *

Eve poured me wine at her place before our dinner with Ted and May. She was busy putting together her outfit as I sat on her living room couch sipping and trying to have a conversation with a women in the throes of deciding what to wear to a fancy dinner. I was wearing slacks, a button up and desert boots. Cleanly shaven, I looked sharp. I told her that whatever she decided to wear, she would make me look like a degenerate.

"You look nice," she said. "Stay the night?" I said I would.

For the evening ahead, I was so curious as to how it would turn out. But I was equal parts nervous. For what, I wasn't exactly sure. There were aspects of my life all about to collide in one night. My love and work life were becoming increasingly intertwined. Perhaps inevitable when choosing to live in a small ski town. Finally, she declared herself ready. I looked at my watch as I poured another round and noticed it was twenty past seven. We had ten minutes to get to the restaurant. Eve didn't think being on time was at all a priority. She grinned while she sipped her wine. I was anxious, prompting her to down her glass. Out the door we went.

Parking outside the restaurant was a nightmare but I managed to find a spot. After six o'clock, free parking in town. I parked awfully close to the person next to me. Eve and I hurried over to Tony's. Ten minutes late. Eve didn't care, whereas I thought this was disrespectful behaviour. We entered the restaurant and a woman took our coats. Eve spotted May and we walked over to their table. They greeted us warmly. Ted poured our glasses full with wine.

Eve's behaviour through the course of the meal was unlike anything I'd seen from her. She behaved like a spoiled brat. The way she didn't like how her broccoli was done, how she figured she had a say in what the next bottle of wine was. I found it off-putting. Ted was of course going to pay for everything. This was the finest, oldest restaurant in Aspen or so I was told. Eve was behaving like she was in a damn Chuck E. Cheese. And the conversation was about nothing. I wanted out of this mess but there was no escape. May kept looking at me like she was a casting director and I was the tenth choice for the role of Eve's boyfriend. Ted meanwhile periodically had to take phone calls, leaving me and the two girls to continue trying to make this situation bearable. Princess Eve was in her element and May soon began slurring. At the end of the whole thing, I felt like nothing was gained. I didn't want to go back to Ted's at all, but they insisted we come.

What really threw a wrench in the evening was a note that was left I discovered underneath my windshield wiper after leaving the restaurant. There was business card paper clipped to it belonging to a woman in the Aspen Police Department. All the note said was to call immediately the number on the card. I did and Officer Judy told me there was a car parked next to me with a fresh scrape on the rear bumper. That I was the one who did it. Judy told me to wait where I was and she would return to file a report. I was shocked and angry at the allegations that I knew were false. I ran over to the other side of my truck and saw the white paint on the rear bumper of the Pathfinder parked beside me. It looked like I had hit the Pathfinder while I was trying to park. I knew that wasn't at all what happened.

Eve overheard my phone conversation. "Lets go," she whined. I hung up the phone and told her I had to wait for the police. Eve said we needed to drive over to Ted's. I said I couldn't just leave now because the police were on their way. It took five seconds for Eve to decide that she was going to leave me there. She phoned Ted to tell him to wait if they hadn't yet left. She was going to ride with them to their house. Officer Judy arrived just as Eve was finishing her call so there was nothing I could do to stop her without making a scene. I was wine buzzed and I didn't want to risk coming across that way to Judy. Eve was drunk. Her obnoxious behaviour, I worried, would make matters more complicated if Judy noticed. Eve left before her behaviour became obvious. Judy and I were left to go over what had happened.

It took an hour before Judy decided that I needed to plead guilty to a glorified parking ticket. She said that there was no way to prove who hit who. The way my truck was parked made it look as though I were the guilty party. Judy said that to make things easier for all parties involved, she would give me a fifty dollar parking ticket. The damage was so small that I thought the whole thing to be ridiculous. Judy said that the guy was angry and called the police because he was unable to get out of the parking stall on account of me parking too close. He told Judy he had a dinner date with his girlfriend and had to run across town to the restaurant in a suit and tie. Give me a break. Judy said she was letting me off and although I was exceedingly polite for the entire process, I shot her a look that said you have got to be kidding me. She saw my New Mexico plates and asked if I was new here. I said I was, and she said "welcome to Aspen." I called Eve for directions as I drove. She said to come to Northstar, east of town on the way to Independence Pass.

I arrived to find Ted, May, and Eve playing cards beside two wine bottles. One empty the other almost. Ted asked if I shouldn't be in jail. This wasn't a place I wanted to be. The only thing that brought me there was the hope Ted would tell me something I didn't know about illegal cigarette distribution. Eve and May both were drunk. Slurring the lyrics to John Denver songs. May said she was friends with Annie back in the day. Ted asked if I wanted to smoke a cigar on the back porch. The house by the way, stunningly beautiful. On the heated porch, we smoked a cigar. I don't like cigars but I smoked anyway. Ted poured me a couple fingers of scotch after retrieving ice from inside. I had sobered considerably from my time spent with Judy. Ted had gone the other way.

"I'm a child of the sixties," he began. "The success of my career, this house, everything was and is predicated on the notion that the US government, be it municipal, state, federal, will overreach. The way they go about convicting supposed drug dealers, I've made a fortune arguing to judges that their tactics are out of Big Brother's handbook." Ted went on like that for a good fifteen minutes. I didn't know why he was saying all this to me. Perhaps it was because he felt like I was going to tell his story regardless and he wanted to position himself in the best possible light. Before I could even ask, he started going into the nitty gritty of the cigarette business.

"You know the key to the whole thing?"

"I don't."

"It's not that the county sheriff is in on it."

"What is it then?"

Ted, grinning: "It's their legal team."

"Right. Using the Westcott Foundation's legal structure for protection...same with Native Reservations... "

"Ha! No. See, that's all a smoke screen. That we set up those legal entities...it's all merely meant to obscure the truth to nosy journalists like you."

"Not what the Arapaho think."

"Oh hell. Sure we haven't been honest with them. But what they don't see is what they are providing us."

"Yeah? How so?"

"You sound skeptical."

"And you're surprised?"

"Look. Law enforcement and prosecutors know that I've been connected to this thing the whole time it's been a going concern."

"How long's that been?"

"God, must be twenty plus years..."

"Long time."

"How old are you? Thirty? Almost as long as you've been on earth."

"There's more to this story than the law simply being broken."

"Of course," Ted said.

"Can I venture a guess?"

"Be my guest," he said as he poured more scotch.

"You want me drunk?"

"Oh fuck, I don't care, don't drink it."

"My guess, this is a way for you to channel information back to the DEA about other illegal activity going on here. Cigarettes? Good money but not great. Compared to cocaine? Heroin? I'm thinking there's information coming out of this whole thing that somehow links to the serious stuff." Ted said nothing.

"You're probably pissed that a guy like Erikson wants to cut out the Sinaloa and source from Asia."

"Kid, you got a good head on your shoulders. The shit I've had to deal with defending the coke dealers of the past here in Aspen, the people I've met, these are all small timers. You're partly right. Guys like Erikson get involved, they think they can overnight make a change to pad their pockets. Erikson got impatient with how much money was being left on the table. What he doesn't get, is we need it to be only tobacco, because once in a while they give up a little piece, a little crumb, of something, anything that helps the government with their case against the big boys. Boring is good. Understand?"

I did. And that was all Ted would say about the whole thing. He flung the scotch out of his glass into the darkness off the porch. He proclaimed he was drunk and that it was time for Eve and I to go. I didn't object. We went inside and I found her and May each sprawled on a couch. They were trying to make conversation about skiing tomorrow. I knew that was not going to happen for anyone. I grabbed Eve by the arm and she slurred something incoherent. I dropped her at her house and didn't bother staying the night. I drove down valley to the horse farm and slept fitfully. I woke at dawn, made coffee, drank a gallon of water and grabbed my skis.

* * *

It was seven when I arrived to a parking stall on the corner of Durant and Hunter. I put my skins on my skis at the truck. This would be the first time for me to skin all the way to the top. I saw a poster advertising a December uphill race to the top of the mountain. That would be a column of mine, absolutely. Up I walked Little Nell, and then up Spar Gulch, and then up 3's lift line.

At the top, I was sweating like I'd ran a New Delhi marathon. Panoramic southern views and endorphins coursing through my blood stream. I recognized Highland Peak, but the name's of most of the surrounding peaks I still didn't know. A ski patroller pointed out Hayden, and said it was where the first Aspen area ski resort was going to be developed in the thirties. A world war got in the way and present day Ajax was where post war developers poured their money. Took me an hour, forty minutes from bottom to top. This would be my new ritual three times at least a week. I could get my time down easy to seventy minutes.

Thinking about last night was a chore given the beauty of Ajax at this hour in the morning. But I had no choice. Ted was propping up the Syndicate as a way to inform the CIA, FBI, DEA. One or all of those agencies. Made sense. But that left me with a moral quandary. What should I do? Make the story public? Talk to Darwin? What good would that do? After last night, I was thinking maybe I should give it all a pass. Just move on with my life, make a comfortable living doing private ski lessons, and enjoy life here in Aspen. Great place for music, food, skiing. Was it in my best interest to jeopardize that life? I could get my instructing certs and teach above the table. I could write a column for the newspaper once a week. I could marry a girl like Eve or Lyons and settle down here. Find a little place in Carbondale or Basalt, live a comfortable life here.

Or I couldn't. I could write the story, and see what would happen. Be the catalyst for change. Maybe change would happen, or not. Forget about working for the New York Times one day, just do it for the sake of people knowing what was going on here. Isn't that what I was here for as a journalist? So what if I ruffled a few feathers. Thompson would roll over in his grave of my choice to not publish the story. Not that I really cared. Still, what would Wolfe do? Did he not make his name on ruffling feathers? I knew what I had to do. Clear as day. I was going to publish the damn thing.

December

In one week, the Coutinho's would arrive from Rio. I hadn't heard anything about Gabriel's wife, so I wasn't sure if there was one. Gabriel and I agreed to meet after they settled into their ski-in/ski-out town house rental at the base of Ajax. God knows how much he was paying for the place during the holidays. This guy had dough. Norman also wanted me to resume my column for the paper's weekly arts and entertainment insert. I was glad to do that, as it would get me out and about. The big to do for me was to finish the Chung piece. I wanted it done, complete, out the door before Gabriel arrived. I wanted to put this chapter of my time in Aspen to a close.

On a Sunday morning, I began to put all my material together and write. It was agonizing. As most of the long stories I am most passionate about are. I was going to write the story in however many words needed. Could be one thousand, two, three, ten. Could be seven hundred.

The opening scene would take place in the jailhouse. The next scene in the past featuring anonymous Eve as a driver. The next scene, quotes from Chung's first lawyer Ari. The next...I wasn't sure. How would I include Erikson and his abrupt departure to Taos? The possible connection it had to financial misappropriation? Native Americans were getting the short end of a deal they shouldn't be involved with. It looked as though all the financial upside was going to a few people like Dianne Westcott, Erikson and Bledsoe. Protective legal cover from an opaque foundation and Native reservations. There was lots to tell. Structure, the most challenging part of crafting a story. I wanted to tell the story in a series of scenes. I wanted it cinematic. This was my kind of New Journalism. Dialogue, scene-by-scene construction, point of view; non-fiction told with brio. Backed up with a paper trail (thanks to Darwin).

I didn't let Norman know what I was up to. All I said to him in a text message was that the Chung piece would be completed and sent to him next Saturday with photos. I didn't say photos though, I said art. What editors like to hear. Norman never replied which was fine by me. My future with the Herald would go in one of two directions. Either my story would be celebrated, or it would cause the paper some serious issues with advertisers and I would never again be published on its pages. Or they could simply kill the story. Or I suppose they could edit the life out of it leaving a document, lobotomized. The more I thought about it, the more I figured they would go with the last option. What was I left to do?

Write one hell of a good story. If Norman decided against publishing it, I could use my instructor earnings to print copies myself to distribute around town. Or just put it online. Or shop it around to other Roaring Fork publications. Thinking about the many ways this thing would eventually surface to the public was a distraction. I had work to do. Balance. I resolved to myself that some semblance of balance was crucial for the story to come out right. I couldn't lock myself in my room and just bang away at the keyboard. The words would go down, but the result would be unsatisfactory. My solution was to skin up either Ajax or Tiehack first thing every morning until the day I pressed send to Norman. I would go before the lifts started spinning. It would get me outside, burn my legs and lungs, and prepare me for the following Saturday's nighttime uphill race event on Ajax. Keep things clear between the ears.

Eve and I had stopped talking. I told her the day after our Thanksgiving dinner with Ted and May, her behaviour was embarrassing. She said I was boring and then I didn't bother speaking to her nor she to me. Our relationship had changed. She had in the short time I'd met her helped me out so much. Whether it was introducing me to Gabriel, Ted, the ski pass, ski tunings, I really did feel indebted to her. But what was I to do? Buy her stuff? I was doing what I could on my end to try and form a meaningful relationship. She needed an axe for her fireplace so I got her one. I couldn't believe she would get her neighbour to chop the wood she bought at a nearby gas station. I chopped her wood. I tried to show her how, but she found swinging an axe terrifying. I was trying to be helpful. But after all was said and done, I wondered whether we were compatible.

At a certain point people become aware of whether they are or not. I am a believer that things can be worked on, things can develop. But I also think that some people, despite their best efforts, just don't mesh. The reasons why, many. Alyssa and I, right now we meshed. I hadn't seen or heard from her in a while, but I had that feeling. As was the case with Lyons. Would more time with either change that? I couldn't know until more time was spent with each of them. I suppose the same could be said about Eve. Time would tell. I sent a message to Alyssa asking her to come by sometime. I was always visiting their places, they should come see me. Alyssa was wild and I liked that. Nothing about her was predictable and that would certainly be the case if she were to come by for a day, evening and night. Alyssa replied a few hours later. "Sure." Nothing more.

I suggested Monday around five and to bring riding clothes. I figured it was time for June to be ridden. I would have Alyssa ride on the horse behind me. It would be incredibly romantic. Out in the Elk Mountains on horseback with a babe. The thought made my agonizing task of writing the Chung piece easier. She said Tuesday. I said that would work great. Faint heart ne'er won fair lady. June and Alyssa and I in the Elk Mountains.

Tuesday came quick. I was in a bad mood all day from a sleepless night. My skin up Tiehack with temperatures around zero didn't help. I couldn't nap afterward, so I powered through the day with coffee and PBJ's. The story was getting the better of me. I felt lost trying to tell it factually and artfully all at once. Alyssa was early to my place catching me by surprise. It was cold and dark and I didn't want to ride June but Alyssa did. She said she had been looking forward to it since I messaged her. I had to follow through with the plan.

I saddled up June and lifted Alyssa onto the horse. She was wearing her ski clothes and I was wearing insulated ranching gear. We would go out behind the house for an hour or two. I would try and get June to gallop. I hadn't ridden a horse in a while and I think that became obvious to Alyssa. After a few minutes of me trying to navigate, Alyssa said "my turn." I didn't object. I was tired and frustrated. Alyssa's presence (and June's) the only bright spot in my day. We awkwardly changed positions on the horse so that Alyssa now had the reigns and I was hugging her waist. It was then that I could smell her perfume. Lilacs. I told her she smelled great and she laughed. "Such a dork," she said.

Alyssa in no time got the horse to a steady trot. And then to a gallop. I will admit, I became nervous. I didn't know if she knew what she was doing. She seemed to be in control but I just wasn't sure. I was holding onto her too tight and she slowed us all down. June was panting, I was sweating, Alyssa was smiling.

I asked: "You done this before?"

"What, ride a horse?"

"Yeah, ride a horse through a forest at a gallop in the snow. You done that before?"

"Nope."

"You're kidding."

"Nope."

"Turn and look at me." She did and I stared at her and she at me. I was thinking she was not going to be able to hold a straight face. But she did and she opened her eyes even more so after a few beats. What could I say?

"Fine, you win. You're crazy."

"How crazy?"

"Plain crazy."

"You sure?"

"I'm just worried I can't keep up."

"Well," she said, "do something about it."

"Like?"

"Act crazy for me," eyes ablaze. I was at a loss. This girl was really something. I felt intimidated, but I felt like there was connection.

"Okay," I said. "My turn."

"No way."

"What do you mean, no way?"

"You're gonna do something stupid if I give you the reigns."

"No I won't. I just want to take us home and take you to my bedroom."

"Pardon me?"

"Need I be more direct?"

"I think I got the point. Be more romantic. And crazy. I dare you."

"Okay, how about you take us home and I make us food and drink and then we explore the roots of our love awash in moonlight."

"Please stop."

But that's what we did. She galloped June home, I fed the mare and put a horse blanket on her. I gave her nose a scratch and she looked at me as if she deserved something in return for what I had coming my way for the rest of the night. I gave her a handful of honeyed oats. Her favourite.

For dinner, I made shrimp scampi. Alyssa lit a joint as I cooked. I was fine with wine. An Italian white I paid too much for. Before I started cooking, I took a shower and Alyssa scared the hell out of me by jumping in as I was shampooing my hair eyes closed. She was so quiet I had no idea she was in there. We made soapy love. While cooking she began talking about her father. I was unsure where this was going but she was saying things that I couldn't tell her not to. Like how much of a jerk he was, about how he used to hit her as a child. The things she started to say, really scary stuff. I couldn't understand why she was bringing this all up now but she was. I stopped her once the entree was ready.

"Not now," I said.

"Then promise to do something about it." I said I would, already tipsy, and most certainly under the spell that is Alyssa.

"Anything you want," I said.

"Good."

And just like that she was back to herself. This girl was trouble. Why was I so attracted? We ate and played cribbage and made love and listened to music and went running outside in the middle of the night stark naked. Donna heard us laughing and shrieking and yelled for us to "shut the fuck up." We laughed harder at Donna's profanity and returned indoors. We fell to sleep naked in bed and when I woke at six, she was already gone. The kitchen clean. I called her later that morning after skinning up Ajax (down to eighty minutes), and she answered by saying that whatever she said last night about her father, she was only kidding. I told her she can't do things like that and she said, "why not? Don't be boring." For the rest of the day, I made significant progress in putting my story together. All I needed to do was include the Darwin documentation, write the ending and for the next two, three days, revise and polish, revise and polish. Later that evening Alyssa messaged me suggesting we hang out Saturday. I said that would be more than okay.

* * *

The uphill race was scheduled for Saturday evening which threw me into a fit of anxiety over how I would skate around double booking my evening. Alyssa wanted to go to Bonnie's and then do après at a new restaurant at the base of Ajax. I had to tell her that Bonnie's wasn't open for another week or two and the new place was doing their soft opening by invite only. "Oh, please," she said. "I can get us in anywhere." I relented and agreed to spend the day with her promising myself that I would sneak out for work and return to her to spend the evening with. But before all that, I had to go to Glenwood. It was time for Darwin and I to have our meeting.

It was nine o'clock at night when Darwin Hamilton and I met in a gas station parking lot off the I-70 in Glenwood Springs. He was in a rush and couldn't stay long.

"Fuckin' Vail Pass took three hours longer than it should've," he said as we shook hands.

"You sure you can't stay for a bite? You're going how much further?"

"Gotta make it to at least Junction tonight. Tomorrow have a meeting in Salt Lake at ten in the morning."

"You want we could meet on your way back through?"

"Could work. I'll let you know. Anyway, here's the binder. All this has been photocopied. Keep it as long as you like. Lotta shit in there."

"Thanks."

"You know the story don't you?"

"To be honest, not really."

"Well, the short of it: Lawyers representing the Westcott Foundation came to our tribe and promised investing in things like new sewer and water lines on some of our reserves. They gave us a huge presentation way back, talkin' like twenty years ago, and promised that if we agreed, not only would they invest in our communities, we'd get dividends from other businesses they wanted to set up through our legal status. It was complicated. Lawyerly. And I'm sure as hell not a lawyer."

"And you agreed?

"Not at first. Seemed too good to be true. But then we heard they were shopping the deal around to other tribes and so we felt like why not? May as well."

"And then what happened?"

"Well, we signed the paperwork, and then that was it. Nothing happened."

"What do you mean?"

"Nothing happened. No money came in. But that didn't stop them from setting up this distribution network you said you're aware of. Started out, it was booze. Then they shifted to tobacco. We didn't know it was happening and we also weren't seeing any cut of the profits they were making. Took years for us to put it all together. They pulled one over on us that's for sure. Anyway long story short, we tried to take them to court..."

"When was this?"

"Nineties. We tried and failed. Tried again, and failed. They got some slick lawyers working for them. It's crazy. It's still happening to this day. They make piles of cash and put us in legal jeopardy over any illegal activity they do. And at no point do we get a penny."

"The name Ted Gaffney ring a bell?"

"Oh sure," Darwin said. "He was the guy set the whole thing up. From Dallas." I didn't bother bringing up my time with Ted on his patio.

"You know anything about their connection with the Sinaloa?"

"Hell, wouldn't be surprised if they're involved. Anyway, look I gotta run. Been on the road for eight hours." We shook hands again, and I thanked him. I left Darwin as he filled his Bronco for a drive to the west.

* * *

Over two weeks had passed since Lyons and I had spoken. When I made that realization, I felt a pang of worry and regret at her being lost to me. The concern I felt was significant enough for me to decide to dash off the ending of the Chung piece and give myself permission to pronounce it complete, despite there being almost two full days before my deadline. Lyons meant something to me and I didn't want to fall victim to He who hesitates.

Thursday at lunch I called her and she picked up after the sixth ring. She sounded small and distant. Preoccupied. I tried to work through what I viewed as a barrier, but nothing was getting through to her. I asked where she was and she said she didn't think it a good idea to tell me. That one stung and it showed in my voice. She relented, and said she was on her way to brunch with a friend who she could tell not to come. I could join instead. Great, I said. I didn't even think to suggest for her to not break her plans. We met for coffee at a new place in town. Lyons wanted for us to work on things together. To give our relationship purpose. She wanted time to decide whether she was interested in a sexual relationship to adjoin our friendship. Our friendship, she thought, came more naturally.

"You never flirt with me," she said.

"Because you don't make yourself available."

"What about the last time we met? When we had coffee in the cafe. It was...awkward."

"You were forty-five minutes late."

"I just, I don't know. Something's missing." This was tearing me up. There was nothing I could think to say to convince her otherwise. "Why don't you give me another chance."

She wouldn't and I left brunch crestfallen. I felt angry. And then I felt it was for the better that she didn't want to be with me because the right girl for me would never behave like this. A bad argument to myself. I was a wreck all day and well into the night. I started texting her late. I tried calling her of course, but she wouldn't pick up. I said that I didn't think we should be friends because I felt in such a way toward her that was all or nothing. And I wanted our relationship to be passionately romantic rather than friendly.

She replied the next morning asking if that last message was in fact true. I said, "sorry babe, it's how I feel." That was partially but not entirely true. In fact I really wanted to be with her, for her to be mine. Self-pity drove me to accept her wishes and to just drop it. Move on, focus my attention elsewhere. I could learn to accept being friends with Lyons and nothing more. It dawned on me soon after, that being the best friend she could ever have would be a chance for me to show my true character. I was doing a Munger inverse and I grinned wide at the pride I felt. Alyssa was all I had left. What mattered was being the best I could be with her to avoid a similar sand through the fingers depression I was enduring with Lyons.

* * *

It took me hours to pour through Darwin's binder. In the end, I put Darwin on record and cited some of the documents that showed the legal framework the Arapaho had agreed to with the Westcott Foundation. I didn't want to lose the reader with too much legalese. So I kept it brief and used Darwin's voice to convey what had happened and how. I chose to end my story in the following way: The narrator is on the porch with Ted who's giving his speech, his plea as to why keeping the scheme afloat was the morally superior course of action. I wasn't going to have a quote be the end of my story so I finished with an artful description of the view from his porch. It went something like this:

Ted finished his closing statement and left me standing there on the porch, empty glass in hand. The pale half moon shone through a scattering of clouds in the northern sky. To the east toward the pass I heard a lone coyote. His call growing louder each passing moment as he chased something toward the outer rim of the Northstar Preserve. It reminded me that out here in the Aspen wilds, every dog for himself.

I thought it was corny and wagered everyone else to read it would too. But what the hell, won't know if I don't try. My decision to include myself in the story did not come easy. Using "I" in non-fiction is nothing more than a tool in my toolkit of literary devices, but it demands for the rest of the story to be told with the utmost truth and integrity. I didn't want my story to be so effortlessly discounted by those whose reputations I no doubt would harm. I didn't want to lose on a technicality. Inserting myself in the story was such a powerful way to turn the story's structure into a narrative and thus more readable. I wanted to pull the reader in and teach her something. You can't break the law in this country no matter what deal with the devil you've made. Simple as that.

My story was ready to send. I sent Darwin a message to tell him we didn't need to meet. I told myself to wait until the actual deadline a day from now before submitting. It would give me time to mull and reconsider certain aspects of the story. Hours later I pressed send anyway. My rationale was that I didn't want this thing hanging over my head while I was with Alyssa tomorrow and while doing the uphill event. If by now there hadn't come any lightning strikes of insight as to how I could improve the thing, that kind of insight likely wouldn't arrive before tomorrow. An elephant leapt off my back the moment I pressed send. I felt like I could jump to the ceiling. I didn't know if the story was any good, but by now I just didn't care. I was ready to make some money teaching kids how to ski and move my attention over to my novel and writing about the wilderness. Old Colorado beckoned.

* * *

Old Colorado. Where was I in this story? I felt lost as I made a pot of coffee in the predawn hours of an early December morning. My scrambled eggs sizzled, the toast was up. Eat before writing. Hunger, a distraction. The disconcerting feeling of being lost, the insecurity of not feeling confident in the task at hand, it gnawed at me to the point of nearly derailing me from continuing on with my story. Somehow I fought through and sat my butt down and started typing. I felt disgust toward myself as I reread what I'd written. It came across as a poor Jim Harrison imitation. Raucous, unironic epistolary stuff. And then there would be sections where I would crib McGuane and then Elmore, and even Hiaasen.

Where was my voice? I was regurgitating the sounds of other voices I'd been reading for years. I suppose it was for my untrained mind the most frictionless way of getting the words down. Getting the words down. Like Lee Child. I read an interview he did once where he was asked where his confidence came in writing his debut novel at the age of forty, after being fired from an executive role in British television. He said being broke and unemployed helped. He also said that he would play a trick on himself by simply faking extreme confidence. It was as simple as that for him to get the words down and write the first of many Reacher books. Child has many millions now in his bank account, twenty odd years later.

So I was working to get the words down. Just get them down, my morning mantra. Sure it would start out by sounding like some strange cocktail of Harrison and Co., but in the back of my head I was hopeful my voice would crack free from its shell much like the evolution of caterpillar to butterfly.

The story's structure so far consisted of the narrator writing a continuous kind of journal entry divided by seasons. The book would take place over the course of two years in the eighteen eighties. Eight parts to the book. Then there would be an epilogue or something that would connect in some loopy way back to the main thesis of the story. What that was, again I wasn't sure. Perhaps it would exist more as a vehicle for entertainment than universal truth. I would be okay with that.

The narrator comes to town from back east. He's in his thirties, is well educated from somewhere like Yale, and has even made it to the Old World cities of London and Paris as a foreign correspondent. His desire to head west into the mountains of America comes from his obsessive reading habit of people like Thoreau and Emerson. He is inspired and thinks his family, immigrants from Scotland, lost their way when after four generations, no one ventured west despite the original patriarch's adventurous spirit getting them across the ocean in the first place. Why had that family fire to seek better through new geography been extinguished?

Lathrop Robertson, my protagonist, was his great-great-grandfather reincarnated. He couldn't live with having a life unlived. He was smart to be aware of people "mining the miners" who wished to find gold and silver in the San Juans, Elks and Sangre de Cristos.

The opening scene would be him seducing a teacher in town married to a prominent mining banker. She was unhappy with her husband's devotion to work and pursuit of fortune. Robertson was not like that at all. He wasn't going to pretend like he deserved something for nothing, unlike the women's husband. A stupid, corrupting hope. Then again Robertson, like all men, liked to think of himself as the singular dog on the block. I wanted to include subject matter that was, as Faulkner said, "raw meat on the floor." Did I even know what that meant? Just get the words down, the words down.

After the woman leaves Robertson's room at the Hotel Jerome, he goes to a court proceeding involving a case concerning misleading assayed mining results from a stake up Midnight Mine. After the court appearance, Robertson travels by horse to interview men who live in Ashcroft, an industry town up the Castle Creek drainage. He needs to put the material together for a story he would wire to a prominent newspaper back east. If the story was of enough importance, he would try to sell his work to several different newspapers across the eastern seaboard. There would even be the occasional time his work would be bought for overseas distribution, in places like London and Dublin.

I wasn't quite sure on the story's narrative arc. I was hoping it would unfold as I got the words down. But my goal was to get this thing to at least sixty thousand words. I didn't want it to take any longer than a month. I would do a minimum two thousand words per day. Before skiing, no matter how tired, frustrated, rushed, or even hungover I may be. Just get the words down.

* * *

I suggested to Alyssa we ski Highlands. She agreed. The Highlands bowl was open and it was sunny. The decision was made for us. She said she'd heard the bowl was in great shape. Crack of noon, we were skiing. The bar at the base was already busy. Young ski racers had gates set on the run in front of us. We rode the first chair, then the second and then booted up to the top of Highlands Peak (elev. 12,393 ft.). That was the first time for me up there and I was charmed by the Tibetan prayer flags flapping in the wind. There were only two others at the top. The cat that moved people from the ski patrol hut to the main gate of the bowl wasn't yet operating. Far less people on the peak.

Alyssa said the best skiing was skier's right. The slope angle she said was over forty. I was impressed she knew slope angles. I sure as hell didn't. I let her go ahead of me after a few moments of contemplative thought atop the mountain. My drying sweat had me soon shivering and I was warmed by the ski down. We skied all afternoon, eating turkey sandwiches I made on a chair ride up. Alyssa had a thermos of baked gaba oolong tea in her backpack. She shared most of it.

What ruined the afternoon was her insistence that we meet friends of hers at the bar at the base of the mountain after we finished skiing. There were four of them and they were already three pitchers deep. There was college football on the bar's TV and the two guys wore football jerseys supporting one of the teams from Ohio. The girls? Heather and Monica. Monica was also friends with Alyssa. And Eve. She therefore knew what I was up to. My heart sank to my feet and she smirked asking why I looked pale. One of the guys shrieked, spilling beer on my ski jacket the moment I sat down. His team hadn't converted on third and two. Had Monica by now told her friends about what I had been doing? If Alyssa did know, how could she have let us have this afternoon together, or the other night at my place? Perhaps this was why Eve and I were no longer much of a going concern. I became neurotic. Of course I would, I was writing a damn novel. Neurosis, reckless behaviour, I fit the archetype.

I lasted for a pitcher of Miller Lite and then abruptly left. I had to make the start of the uphill race. My mistake was that I had failed to mention my participation in it to Alyssa the whole day. My own damn fault. Now it looked like it was obvious I knew what they knew. But did they know? I know one of them did. But did Alyssa?

I was a mental wreck the entire bus ride over to Ajax. It was cold, dark, not even six at night. Did I really want to walk to the top? No, but I would do it and eat a big plate of whatever they were serving once I reached the top. I would ski down without a headlight in the pitch black. I would somehow try and forget about the imminent collapse of the house of cards that was my love life in Aspen. I was ruined. Every-one in town would hear of what an asshole I was. No self-respecting woman would choose to go near me. I was the grinch with a bombshell of a story about to be published that would no way make me any new friends. How much longer could I last in Aspen? The whole enterprise of me being here, a ticking time bomb.

Once I got to the start line I was glad I was there. Looking around, these were my kind of people. Not entirely my crowd but halfway there. People that liked going under the rope. What I was noticing though, and perhaps this was solely a reflection that I was in Aspen, was the quality of equipment everyone had. All my stuff was used and cheap and barely hanging on. This crowd had the best of the best of ev-erything. When the horn went to start the race, I quickly got ahead of plenty of A-type looking guys with thousands of dollars worth of skis and boots and backpacks and skins. I wasn't doing this to race, I was just doing it to meet people, have a good meal at the top. There was an all you can eat buffet waiting. The full moon was my headlamp.

At the top I was drenched with sweat. Seventy-five minutes bot-tom to top. Not bad. Down would take me no more than five minutes, so I took my time up there relaxing and eating plenty of food. Lasagna and steamed vegetables and beer and cake and cookies for dessert. I sat with strangers until I noticed Norman was sitting across the room. He was with his wife Maria whom I'd yet to meet. I walked over to say hello and see if they minded me joining them. They didn't. Maria and I finally were introduced. I looked at Norman. "Thought you never skied?"

"We don't. Rode the gondola up for the food." Immediately he brought up my story. "We're going to publish it around Christmas time because it's damn time this whole thing is brought to light." I didn't think this was at all how Norman was going to respond. "There were parts I had to cut, the fluffy stuff, but for the most part I kept it all," he said. "I liked your scenes, but sometimes wondered whether using 'I' was the right thing to do."

"This is going to cause a shitstorm but I will go to bat for you so long as what you've written is factual. We don't have the budget for fact-checkers, so I will have to take your word for this being accurate and ethical." I told him it was the most honest thing I'd ever written.

The whole time Norman was talking, his wife was looking at me with a sort of detached worry. I am sure she was glad that it was my name that would be going in the byline as opposed her husband's, as it once upon time used to always be. This wasn't her first rodeo. But it was mine and I felt like Norman was raising the stakes. I had to stand tall, chin up. I wasn't really in this business to make friends out of everyone. Was I doing nothing more than picking a fight? Maybe I was overanalyzing the whole thing. I left the Norman's after wolfing down a couple plates of food. I Chinese downhilled it top to bottom, in the dark. It was exhilarating and exactly what I needed. Took me four minutes, eighteen seconds.

When I got out of the bus at Buttermilk, I checked my phone charging in the dash. It died from me exposing it to the cold night air. When it booted up, I saw Alyssa had tried calling three times. She left voicemails and sent text messages. Something was up. I didn't bother reading or listening to anything before calling her. She picked up on the first ring. She wanted me to come to her place as soon as I could. Before I could say anything, she hung up the phone.

When I got to her door, I was nervous. She was going to end it all right here and I would be left to scurry my way back down to Carbondale, tail between my legs. Eve and Alyssa, both out of my life. Lyons wanting nothing more than friendship. How soon fortunes can change. Alyssa opened the door. She looked terrific and the thought of her eventual abandonment induced in me a wave of remorse. She invited me in, avoiding eye contact. I took my shoes and coat off and followed her through the living room to the little room next to her kitchen. She sat down in a chair and I sat in one across from her. Her eyes, teary.

"Alyssa, I'm sorry." She said nothing.

"I only just met you, so I wasn't sure what we were yet. I'm new here, it can be lonely." Nothing.

"If it means anything, I am totally transfixed by you and I want to spend all my time with you and only you."

"Bullshit," she said.

"It's true."

"I thought I could trust you?"

"You can."

"How am I to believe that? It can't be based on past behaviour."

"I know. But you can. I promise."

"Trust does not come easy with me."

"One of the many reasons I'm drawn to you."

"And the others?"

"What, reasons?"

"Yeah. Go on, tell me the reasons why."

"You're the most fearlessly spontaneous person I've ever met."

"That all?"

"No. You're smart, sarcastic, beautiful...I could go on."

"Please do."

"You ride a horse really well, you eat my cooking, you..."

"Are generous with letting you into my life."

"Yup. Another reason." We talked for a long time. Alyssa was rightfully upset. Eventually: "You can leave now...I need time to think."

"Okay. Alyssa, again...I am truly sorry. I want to be with no else except for you and you can trust me when I say that." She said nothing.

"I'll be leaving now."

"Go."

"Bye."

* * *

I left her place shaking. What kind of animal was I? I let temptation get the better of me. I was on a cross that only I could bear. My skin felt like it was on fire and my face, completely numb. I walked off balance toward my truck. I checked my phone and felt a compulsion toward calling Eve and explaining myself. I went so far as to even dial her number, but it was fear that stopped me. I drove all the way back to the horse farm with tears streaming down my face. I needed to do better. I was behaving in a way that ran counter to the way I was raised.

My mother would say, "one of the last things your father said to me before he was killed in Desert Storm was to make sure you treat women like an officer and a gentlemen." She would say that anytime the subject of women would come up through my entire childhood. And still to this day. That was all I needed to do. What had happened? I felt sick and went straight to bed and slept deeply for eleven straight hours. When I woke I felt disoriented. It was light out, birds were chirping and I could hear someone or something making noise in my kitchen. I didn't give it much that thought there was someone or something else in my place. Clumsily, I walked into the kitchen in my underwear. I was half asleep, I could barely see straight. Standing over a pot of coffee was a young woman.

"Alyssa?"

"The other one."

Sheepishly: "Eve?"

"Her too?"

"Lyons?"

"Hi."

"Hi." I went over to the sink, splashed cold water on my face. I could see clearly again.

"I need some help," I said.

"You sure do."

"Now you know there were two others."

"I had a feeling."

"Of course you did. How could I think otherwise?"

"You're male."

"I tried to make amends last night to Alyssa. I don't know if she even knew I was there at her house."

"I don't know her but I know Eve. You need to talk to her. She's in the other room."

"She's here?"

"Eve!" Eve appeared from the mudroom. She looked calm, composed.

"Should've known," she said.

"I mean it wasn't like we were seeing each other for that long?"

"Long enough in my book. Can't believe you're trying to get out of this."

"I'm sorry."

"Are you?"

"Yes. I just...I don't know. I didn't think we were clicking."

"The whole time? That's how long I was told you were seeing her. And her," she said looking in Lyons' direction. I was speechless.

"Guys like you don't last long here in Aspen," Eve said.

"Eve, I am sorry."

"I told Ted."

"Why'd you do that?"

"He was curious as to why I was crying yesterday at après." At après. Give me a break.

"Eve. I am so, so sorry."

"We're done. Ted is gonna make your life hell."

And then the two former lovers of mine left. Didn't even close the door. Took my pot of coffee with them too. Where would I find a replacement carafe?

* * *

That evening Gabriel met me in his palatial townhouse after he texted to say they'd arrived and settled. My day was a wash the moment the girls left. Some officer, some gentlemen. The sight of Gabriel's adorable little girls gave my soul a glimmer of hope. I would right my wrongs by teaching these little girls the best I could. Not just skiing but a rigorous moral code to use on the mountain and in life. These two girls became the object of my focus for righting my wrongs. Writing Old Colorado would fall in that category too. Teaching and writing and reading. That was my next three, four weeks. Simple. I felt inspired by the simple task in front me: teaching kids how to ski properly. I was getting paid way too much for such a simple thing but then it was nice to know that my skillset would for the first time be generously compensated. My entire professional career was predicated on the notion that the things I enjoyed doing, writing and teaching skiing, were not valued in the marketplace. To me, it's arbitrary how occupations are compensated.

A young woman in her twenties greeted me at the door of Gabriel's. I arrived to the Residences at the Little Nell and was led to his rental by a guy working the front desk. It was a maze finding the right door but eventually we found it. The young woman barely said hello but let me in and went back to whatever she was doing on her iPad in the far corner of the room. I sat on a couch in the high ceilinged living room marvelling at how some people live. Gabriel appeared walking quickly down a staircase. He looked nothing like I thought he would. Tight washed jeans pre-ripped at the knees. A white baggy sweater that said APRÈS in bold blue lettering. What hair he had left was cut close to to his head. Cleanly shaven. He looked like a rich obnoxious ski tourist. He was fit for Aspen.

Gabriel sat across from me on the couch and we went over the next few weeks. I would meet his girls at the base of the Aspen gondola and take them skiing from half past nine in the morning to three in the afternoon. Everyday. Gabriel spoke in a quietly even voice. His English was perfect, his Brazilian accent slight. He made no mention as to who the young girl was sitting thirty feet away from us. She didn't say one word the whole time I was there. I asked Gabriel what kind of skiers his girls were. The eldest, age fourteen, he said was a "great skier." Her name, Marcia. The younger of the two, age twelve, "needed some work." Her name, Francisca.

Gabriel wondered how I would like to be paid and I said however many days we end up doing we would tally it all up at the end before their departure and a wire transfer would work just fine. I asked if they were jet lagged. He said no because before arriving, they spent a week in Los Angeles at a friend's place in the Palisades. We shook hands, I left.

The next morning, I took the girls straight over to Ruthie's on the west side of Ajax. We skied groomers all morning. I didn't even instruct. I just wanted them to get used to being on skis again. The last time they skied was on their previous winter vacation in St. Moritz. Marcia and Francisca spoke perfect English. In the brief time I had come to know this family, they came across as more anglo than I ever would've imagined Brazilians to be. The girls said they were on school break right now from their private all girls school. They went to an English school in Rio and wore uniform. They were shy and proper. I was trying all morning to loosen up the mood but there was nothing I could do to break the ice. For lunch we all had grilled cheese sandwiches at the top of the mountain. They each only ate half a sandwich. They paid with cash their father had given them. Marcia was the money handler and took out a roll of hundred dollar bills. The grilled cheese sandwiches and hot chocolate perked the girls up and we had a better time in the afternoon.

We skied groomers off lift's 3 and 8. We went over to check out 1A before the end of the day. Their accommodation was as ski-in/ski-out as anyone could possibly get. The girls politely said thanks, left their skis on the racks designated for guests and walked through the doors. Gabriel let me use his parking stall in the underground garage. They didn't need a vehicle while in Aspen because the concierge would take them anywhere they pleased in big black SUV's. I was given a key for the garage that also worked on the doors the girls used to reenter the building. I waited until they were gone before entering the same doors. There was a full spread of après snacks and beer and wine for guests. I helped myself and went down to my truck and drove home. This was a cushy gig. Thank you, Eve. Thinking of her, it hurt. Gabriel sent a message asking how the day went. I said great. The girls' skiing was mediocre but I didn't tell their father. Gabriel sent back a thumbs up emoji.

The first few days went the same. The girls were shy and didn't say much and just did what I said. They didn't care where we went skiing and barely ate or drank at lunch. It was a bit off, the whole thing. Gabriel suggested late one evening that we all go for a ski the next day. I said that would be fine, thinking he meant he and I and the two girls. He said to meet them at the top of Snowmass for lunch at a newly opened restaurant and then we would all ski Snowmass for the rest of the afternoon.

* * *

Gabriel and the girls including the young woman who greeted me at the door were sitting at a table waiting for me when I arrived. I was on time so didn't feel the need to apologize. Gabriel finally introduced the young lady, her name Ana. I assumed she was a young mother and, as I sat down, said to her she had pleasant daughters. Everyone laughed. She said, "You think I'm their mother?"

"Their mother is in Rio," Gabriel said. "Ana's my girlfriend."

"Oh, I'm sorry."

"It's okay," Ana said. "You're not the first person." Gabriel ordered the adults champagne and then shots of peppermint schnapps. His way of breaking the ice. We all ordered soup and Gabriel kept ordering booze.

Our table grew livelier and when Ana said halfway through our meal she was going to go to the bar to get us more schnapps, Gabriel laughed.

"You're only nineteen," he said.

I nearly choked on the chicken I was chewing. Nineteen? A rich guy in his fifties with two adolescent daughters dating a girl aged nineteen? Who were these people? Never had I met a family anything like this.

By the time we left the restaurant it was half past one and we were all fairly drunk save for Marcia and Francisca. What prompted us to finally leave and quit eating and drinking was Francisca stealing her father's phone and laughing while showing us photos he had stored. The photos were of Ana nearly naked, in a G-string, sipping champagne in their bathroom. Too much information. Gabriel's face reddened but he didn't really scold his daughter. It was all one big joke. Gabriel said we'd better get skiing to which I said absolutely. I needed to get out of this place. Ana, the most inebriated, demanded that I get us all some shots "for the road." I declined saying we'd all had enough. She raised her voice and called me a "soft cock." I laughed at first but she kept saying it until finally I looked at her stone cold and said, "Behave."

We left the place and I felt bad for Marcia and Francisca. What kind of model were Gabriel and Ana for them? They were such sweet girls and I wondered how they couldn't go through episodes like what had just happened without being affected. Ana and Gabriel wore Prada ski outfits. Gabriel's was bright orange and Ana's, yellow. The amount of money spent at lunch, over a grand. Bottles of Veuve Clicquot, expensive food and round after round of schnapps. Ana could barely get herself down the mountain. Today was the third day ever for her on skis. Gabriel was laughing at her as she kept falling. I tried to help but she kept calling me a soft cock, so finally I gave up and skied with Marcia and Francisca to the bottom.

My truck was parked down the road a few miles. Gabriel insisted he give me a ride to my truck. When Ana and Gabriel finally made it down, Ana's cockiness was completely gone from the horror of what she'd just had to do. Waiting for us was a black SUV from the concierge. We all piled in and by now it was four in the afternoon. We got one run in. But I was getting paid nine hundred bucks so what did I care. Gabriel demanded the driver to change the station from the quiet jazz playing. There was nothing on the radio he liked. Gabriel connected his phone to play his own music. Post Malone at max volume, windows rolled down.

It was a short ride to where my truck was parked, thank God. I felt nauseous. When they let me out, Gabriel told the driver to "haul ass" and they peeled out of the parking lot; Post Malone blasting. The whole afternoon was unlike any I'd ever experienced. Gabriel told me he worked in wealth management. I wondered who would give their money to a guy like him, but then maybe his home life was the complete opposite of what I'd just witnessed. I wondered what the mother of his children was like. I wondered if she had any idea who Ana was.

* * *

The next day I skied with the girls on Ajax. They acted like nothing happened the previous day. It was only a couple weeks before Christmas and all they wanted to talk about was the presents they hoped to get. I had sent Gabriel a message telling him to make sure the girls had all mountain skis for the day. Seven inches of fresh snow had fallen overnight. Time to learn to ski powder. Bonnie's was open for lunch, with their famous pancakes and white bean chilli and baking.

The girls were horrible at skiing powder. They had no idea how to do it. It took all morning for me to show them the right way. They defaulted to skiing on their heels after I'd made it clear to them to be on the balls of their feet. With knees bent and hands where they could see them. When they finished their turn, I told them they must pole plant to initiate the next turn. Not a pole touch, a plant. They had to mark their territory, all the way down like they were planting a flag on the moon. They listened politely but couldn't take in what I was telling them and incorporate it into their skiing. They would fall in the powder, laugh and make snow angels. It took us all morning to do three runs. My heart broke as I saw other people absolutely shredding run after run. Face shots of snow with each turn. I was not getting any of that. I had sold my skiing soul to Gabriel.

At lunch in Bonnie's it was a beehive of activity. I got the feeling that anyone who was anyone in Aspen was there. A powder day on Bonnie's season opener. I ordered a bowl of white bean chilli, pizza and a slice of apple strudel. I asked the woman who gave me my strudel why it was famous. She told me while heaping on a spoonful of homemade whip-cream that it was the same recipe the original owner of the place used from back in the fifties. Back when the place was called Gretl's. "Try it," she said. "You'll love it." I took a sample bite and agreed. This would not be my last slice of strudel.

Somehow we found a table in the crowded place. I sat down, exhaling. My mind had me thinking I deserved a break. I didn't need a break. I was on the side of a mountain in fresh powder for close to two hours telling polite young girls how to ski. And here I was about to eat gourmet food. And I was being paid nine-hundred bucks. I smiled to myself thinking this was too good to be true. My financial life for the past eternity, a constant struggle. To think, some people have millions. I was having an internal celebration for my forthcoming status as a thousand-aire.

I looked up from my strudel and staring right at me from across the room was Harry Garr. Seated next to him was Alyssa, a couple of her friends and an old ski instructor. My heart started racing. Garr didn't look happy to see me. Neither did Alyssa or the ski instructor seated next to her. Did the instructor somehow know I was teaching kids under the table? I could get in serious trouble if the resort found out what I was doing. Did Garr know about the story I had submitted? How much had Alyssa told him of what I'd been up to? I walked over to Garr and told Marcia and Francisca I'd be back in a minute.

To Garr, I asked: "You see something you like?" I didn't even look at Alyssa, her two friends or the instructor.

Garr said, "When's it going to be published?"

"When the editor decides he wants it published."

"So you wrote it."

"I sure did." We held each other's gaze.

Finally, the ski instructor: "Those girls paying you?"

"What girls?"

"Oh please. I know exactly what you're doing. Privates."

"And who are you?" I was curious to know.

"Jean Valdene. Senior ski instructor Aspen Mountain. Forty-five years."

"It shows."

Valdene looked at Garr: "Who is this guy?"

"My name ie Meko Torres, nice to meet you. Those girls over there? Family friends. I don't charge friends for instruction. Is Harry a friend?

"Forty-five years."

"Harry, is Jean charging you?

"None of your business," Jean said.

"I bet Jean still has you doing the reverse shoulder. Harry, the story is going to be published whether you like it or not."

"It's a cheap shot," said Garr. "Just like how you got my photo the other night at my place."

"Had to do it."

Nothing more was said and I returned to my table. It stung. I was now on the wrong side of Harry Garr. But really, what did I care? Here was an old crank resting on the laurels of work he did over forty years ago. Alyssa never said a word. I was proud of the way I handled the situation. What was she doing sitting with those fossils anyway? Marcia and Francisca asked what happened. They laughed after I told them about my crazy night at Garr's. They wondered who he was. In the sixties, I told them, he was Hollywood's hottest director. I listed some of his movies and both girls had no idea. To them, Garr was two hundred years old. I looked toward Alyssa. She wasn't laughing over there. Here I was in a role she probably didn't think me capable of. The responsible, capable, caretaker. I felt sorry for her. Marcia and Francisca rightly guessed that Alyssa and I had dated. They said I could do better which I thanked them for saying. In the afternoon, we did two runs in two hours and that was our day.

* * *

Driving home, an email came from Norman. He said we needed to talk about my story. I pulled over and called him right then and there. I wanted to know immediately what was on his mind. He said he knew I would call as soon as I saw the email.

"What's up Norm?"

"We need to talk about your story."

"Go on."

"Somehow word got out that we were going to publish a story about this whole thing..."

"And...?"

"And I've been getting a tonne of pressure..."

"To do what? Don't tell me."

"No I'm not going to kill your story."

"Lobotomy?" Norman said nothing. "Let me guess, Harry Garr called the publisher and started bitching?"

"Not just him, others too. Can't say who because I honestly don't know."

"Let me guess, Bledsoe, Ted Gaffney, I bet Ari even called in. I wonder if Chung knows what's going on."

"You didn't hear?"

"Hear what?"

"Chung made it back to Korea yesterday. Ted pulled something."

"No kiddin'."

"He's gone Meko."

"I bet Erikson was bitching about the whole thing too."

"Wouldn't doubt it. Anyway, if I don't tone down your story, it's my job that could be on the line. And while you may think it's easy to 'do the right thing,' talk to me when you have a mortgage and tuition for two kids in college to pay for."

"This is exactly why I need to quit journalism." Norman said nothing. "And write novels...are you serious about all this?"

"You done?"

"Well how much are you gonna winnow it down?"

"I'll send you a revised copy tonight. Let's meet on Monday and go over it."

I put my face in my hands. I was so angry at the whole thing, because I knew that whatever Norman was going to send me, it would be diluted to the point where anyone could have written it. A bone with no meat. I turned my truck around. Back to Aspen. To a bar, any bar. I didn't have any bros to drink with as all my energies had been focused on chasing skirts, working and exercising the past two months.

At the Red Onion I ordered beer and whiskey. Norman's email came. I read the revised copy and almost puked. I was sitting at the bar in no mood to talk to anyone. So I kept drinking. Shots and beer. After an hour of trying to talk to bartenders, I called Gabriel but there was no answer. I sent him a message asking him to meet for a drink. No reply. I felt compelled to reach out to one of Alyssa, Lyons or Eve, but I knew each option was a dead end. Secretly I was hoping one of them would text me but no message came. I was blitzed inside of ninety minutes of arriving to the Red O and was sick of the place.

Where to go next? I couldn't drive home so I went to see if anyone was playing the Belly Up. I was in luck. Tonight's show, the Wood Brothers. A scalper sold me a ticket for eighty bucks. I ordered a cheeseburger and waited for the sold out show to begin. Sure enough, there was Lyons near the front of the stage. I saw her before she saw me. I ate my food and went to where I would've anyway for a show like this. By the stage. These guys could play. I tapped Lyons on the shoulder and she turned. She was standing next to a guy whispering in her ear. Her face lit up at the sight of me and gave me a hug. I didn't expect this kind of reception. She grabbed my hand and led me to one of the bars in the back. I said this round was on me and she ordered two shots of tequila. I was drunk and didn't think twice saying no.

"Drunkern shit," I slurred.

"Can tell. Need a place to crash?"

"You'd be okay with that? What about him?"

"Who?"

"Whisperer guy."

"Derek?"

"Yeah. Derek." Lyons laughed. She was hearing jealousy in my slurred speech.

"Just a friend. Like you."

"Oh, okay. You sure you don't mind?"

"This is Aspen, silly."

I thanked her. We walked back to where she was standing when I found her. Right in front of the stage. The show started and, wow. Like I said, these guys can play. The musicianship, outstanding. The lead vocals a bit nasally but it was a damn good show. After, Lyons invited me to join her group of friends. I went along. This was really my first night out on the town. Not since Montana had I made a habit of hard drinking and staying out till four before devouring late night pizza. Tonight was going to be one of those nights. Marcia and Francisca would have a hungover instructor in the morning.

* * *

I woke up at five in the morning fully clothed next to Lyons in her bed. I felt like I'd had no more than ten minutes sleep. I tried for more rest. Not happening. I tossed and turned for an hour before Lyons demanded I get out of the bed. Only then did I notice she was naked. I could not remember if we'd done anything and neither I nor her was in any mood to talk. The room temperature must've been in the nineties;

a good explanation for her sleeping nude. I was sweating. I got out of her bed and felt like dying the moment I stood up. This was going to be a long day. I remembered then why I no longer boozed it up like I used to. I couldn't eat, but I drank a gallon of water and four cups of coffee.

I left Lyons' place at seven and went to look for my truck. I couldn't remember where it was. Aimlessly, I wandered. I started at the Red Onion. Must be near there and sure enough it was. I changed into my ski gear and walked back to where I could drink unlimited coffee in the lobby of Gabriel's hotel. As soon as I sat down with my cappuccino, I fell asleep. It was Francisca who woke me by poking my forehead, giggling. She was wearing pyjamas.

"You smell," she said.

"Ready to ski?" I said, dazed.

"Marcia's knee is sore and I feel sick, my dad tried to call you but you weren't answering. We aren't skiing today." The relief I felt was enormous. I was instantly able to think and see a little clearer and only then did I notice the rest of the family seated a few feet away laughing, eating their breakfast.

"How long you guys been there?"

"Half an hour. You started to snore, dad thought I should wake you."

Relief was displaced by embarrassment. I looked over to Gabriel and there he was eating a cinnamon bun, waving and smiling.

"Yikes," I said.

"I think maybe you need a day off too?"

"Yeah I feel kind of sick myself."

"Flu?"

"Must be."

I got up and said hello to the family. Ana was laughing the hardest and said I was no longer a soft cock.

"We saw you last night but you didn't see us. You were crazy."

"Was I?" My embarrassment wasn't going anywhere. "I think I need to get some sleep."

"Goodnight Mr. Torres," Gabriel said, laughing. I smiled. What else could I do? They didn't even know I was a journalist. That fact about me had never come up so they had no idea what kind of drama I had in my life. A life designed to be as undramatic as possible. I went back to Lyons' and crashed beside her in her bed. My abrupt entrance startled her awake.

"Meko? Aren't you supposed to be skiing?" I was asleep before I could answer.

* * *

Monday morning I was back to being me. The night before I asked Norman if we could meet at his office at eight to which he agreed. I had gone to bed at eight and slept till seven. I woke up feeling as if Saturday night never happened. Lyons and I did not in fact make love in the wee hours. She made sure I knew that. It was a new reality between us that I was capable of accepting. When I finally left her place at two in the afternoon, I said: "Goodbye dearest friend." She laughed.

At the Herald office, Norman and I had our meeting in a depressingly drab conference room. He looked like he hadn't slept. "You know, I haven't been sleeping," he said as he sipped his coffee.

"Really? I got eleven hours last night."

"Charmed life. Listen, I've been reconsidering this whole thing. I want to publish the version you sent with only a couple revisions."

"Really? What about tuition and mortgages and—"

"My wife has rich parents. We'll be okay."

"You sure? I mean there was some acidic stuff I wrote in there."

"You want me to change my mind?"

"No, I just...you sure?"

"Meko, We can't get pushed around like this. What's the point of this whole enterprise if we can't write the truth?"

"I agree."

"We are going to publish your story but what my publisher is insisting is that at the end, there will be a one sentence disclaimer type thing saying the views expressed are independent of the paper."

"So, it's going to be run like an opinion piece?"

"Letter to the editor."

"Well, better than nothing. But no doubt people will just discount it as some crank writing from his mother's basement."

"Better than nothing," Norman said.

"This is true. Okay, that it?"

"Yes. It will run Saturday the 27th. You think Aspen's busy now? Wait till after Christmas. I want to tell this story to as many people as we can. Front page. Despite it being presented as a letter."

"Thanks Norm."

"Oh and I need you to do for me some more Christmas party coverage. That okay?"

"So long as the events are at night or on Ajax mountain that's fine. I have family friends in town right now and I promised I would ski with them every day until the first week of January."

"That's fine. Just give me some good material."

"Fine by me. Keep me posted on any Christmas happenings. Not really my scene."

"Can you go to the snow polo event next week?"

"Sure."

"Great. Now go teach those foreign kids how to ski. That's the only way you're gonna afford to live here."

"How'd you know?"

"Aspen's small," Norman said grinning. "I thought by now you'da figured that out."

I walked out of there feeling electric. Today was Monday. The story would go out on Saturday. What would my world be like a week from today? Would I be run out of town? That was a real concern for me and if that were to in fact happen, down the drain would all that money go from not skiing with Gabriel's daughters for the rest of their stay. I was surprised at how much I'd come to like boujee Aspen. Nine hundred bucks a day. I needed to let Gabriel know in advance what was going on in my life and decided to tell him after skiing. I sent him a message asking him if he could meet me for a beer at the end of the day. Not just for fun but to talk business. He got back to me right away and asked if his daughters were misbehaving.

"No no, I just need to let you know about something that could prevent me from skiing with them."

"Okay," he said. "See you after skiing."

Today, I wanted to show Marcia and Francisca the thrill of ski racing. So, all day I stood on the side of Ajax's public ski race course and coached the girls through the giant slalom gates. They had butter knives for edges and were slipping and sliding around each gate, but they were having a blast. I waited for them at the bottom of the course to coach them on how to improve their racing technique. After each run, their eyes were aglow with curiosity and ambition. Who knew these two had a racing streak in them; especially Francisca. They weren't fast and looked terrible skiing through the gates, but they were loving it.

It reminded me of when I used to love to race. Before my college racing days, before my senior high school racing days, before all of that. When I was a ten, eleven year old. That period of my ski racing history was the best and the joy I got from those two years propelled me as far as I eventually went in the sport. I suppose it's a personal tragedy how I lost the love for the sport. I was too driven and the politics of who was chosen for the national team farm system, all of that garbage I now see as wasted energy. When I threw a punch at one of my coaches in my second to last year of NCAA eligibility, that was the final straw for me and what got me kicked off the team and out of the sport.

Here's what happened. Our coach Franz was clearly in bed with one of the girls on our team and I called him out about it one day in front of the whole team and other teams too. We were racing in Vermont and it was an important qualifier for US championships. Breanna and her little clique were getting all the attention from the coach. It was their schedules our coach worked around. The guys and I were left to set our own courses, do all the work. It was ridiculous. But this guy had coaching pedigree from Austria and had coached Austria's top men in the nineties. He was treated as ski racing royalty. No one talked back to him.

I finally had enough and tore into him just as the women were about to start their race. We swung punches at each other in the damp, cold Vermont air. Parent volunteers pulled us apart. In the end, Franz got off on account of his sterling reputation, his lover made it to the national team and I was in ski racing exile. I was able to finish my degree but I was so fed up with ski racing that I never said one word of protest at my dismissal. Had I instead blown both my anterior cruciate ligaments and been forced out of the sport that way, I wouldn't have cared. I was ready to move on.

Near the end of the day, Marcia and Francisca insisted I race them both in the dual course. I was reluctant but eventually gave in. I let them both win and we skied down to the bottom pretending we were downhill racers. I taught them how to properly do a ski racing tuck for aerodynamics. Francisca surprised me at how natural skiing fast came for her. Gabriel had the money, so I figured I'd tell him that he should put her in a ski racing program while they were on their annual five week winter vacation. Marcia, I could see would be better suited to focus on skiing the black diamonds, mogul runs, the off-piste. She had more of a care-free spirit and was fine skiing just for the sake of being outside in the mountains, sans competition. I could identify with the contrasting qualities between the sisters.

By now, they had let their private school guard down and couldn't help teasing me from the moment we started skiing to the end of the day. They wondered if I was dating anyone, told funny stories of their dad and Ana, told of school drama back home. They began to act like normal girls so far as I was concerned. I asked about their mother and

Marcia said they didn't see much of her. "She spends most of her time with her boyfriend in Sao Paulo. We never really hear from her." There was a trace of sadness in Marcia's voice. It was hard for me to hear. The relationship I had with my own mother was the complete opposite and it struck me then how lucky I was to have a mother like my own. In some strange way Gabriel reminded me of her. He was crazy but so obvious was his love for his daughters. Why couldn't my mom make his kind of money?

* * *

To Gabriel over beers I said, "I never told you, but I also work as a freelance reporter here in town."

"You write about...avalanches?"

"There's actually more going on here than you might think."

"Where the next fundraiser is?"

"Done yet? This story...it could force me out of town."

"What's it about?"

"There's some corruption and money laundering that's been going on far too long in this town."

"You're talking to me as if this kind of stuff never happens. Meko, I'm from Rio."

"Bad down there?"

"Don't ask how I make my money."

"I've been curious."

"Like I said, don't ask. My girls, they have no idea what it took for me to give them this life," Gabriel said looking around the barroom, motioning with his free hand toward the snow covered slopes. A local band of Mississippi transplants were about to start a set on the outside patio.

"I gotta say, the way you parent, unlike anything I've ever seen. They said to me the other day you take your helicopter instead of driving to your country house when it gets too hot."

"We live a good life."

"Anyway, when this thing is made public, I may have to leave town on account of my own safety. There are some unsavoury dudes whose livelihoods I will be putting in jeopardy."

"Let me know how I can help?"

"Thanks, but that's really not why I am telling you this. I just don't want you to wonder why I'm not showing up to ski with your daughters each morning."

"Just let me know if you end up leaving, I will understand. I really only wanted my girls to ski with someone so as to get them out of their shell. When their mother left us, it really hit them hard. I worry about Marcia in particular. She's at a tender age for her parents to split like we did."

"Francisca by the way should try out ski racing. She's a natural."

"I'm not surprised. She competes at everything. First one to finish dinner, first one to get her homework done. But she's good natured about it. Marcia, she's more creative, more of an artist. Has she shown you photos of her drawings?"

"No! I'll make sure I ask though."

"She's really talented. Anyway, Meko if you need help with anything, just let me know. I can't promise anything, but I like you. I like how you've taken care of my daughters. Just let me know." We downed our beers and parted ways.

* * *

Holiday streets of Aspen. Packed with shoppers. Rich people spending fortunes on designer handbags, ski suits, abstract art, anything and everything. Later that evening, I convinced Eve to go out for a thank-you dinner for introducing me to Gabriel. I wanted to give her a Christmas gift. I set off looking for something she would like. I had no clue, so I started rambling like a tourist from store to store. I didn't have the kind of money to buy her most of what I was looking at but I thought it was funny pretending to sales associates I was an interested buyer. It took me two hours of walking around Hyman, Mill, Durant before I found a little shop selling vintage East Asian items.

The owner was busy helping an older Southern couple. They were pestering the owner with questions about what it was like in Hong Kong and Singapore and what celebrities were in town. "Gwyneth was in here just the other day," she said without any trace of emotion. The older couple thought that was pretty nifty. They paid and left. The owner asked if I needed any help. I asked her how her day was going, handing her earrings I found. "I am so over Aspen. These people, they take two hours of my time asking questions like what celebrities are here. I am OVER it."

"Gwyneth?"

"Ha! They'll believe anything. When you say things like that, people buy more."

"I mean if she's a customer..."

"Exactly."

* * *

Eve and I went for sushi. I told her about her gift, about how I got it at a place A-listers like to shop. She wasn't going for it and laughed. I knew she'd do that. I spent two hundred bucks on our meal. Roll after roll. I told her I may have to leave town soon and she looked at me without much emotion. "Too bad," she said. I was aware that I didn't deserve much more from her, but at least I tried to make peace. She liked the earrings and put them on at our table. She was wearing a hat she had custom made from a store in town. Eve was Boheme mountain chic to a tee. As we walked out of the restaurant she grabbed my hand saying it was a sign of friendship.

"I think I might actually miss you if you leave. Imagine that."

"So there's at least one person that might."

"Norman will. He loves you."

"We'll see how much he misses me if he loses his job over this."

"You know, your origin story here is unlike anyone I've ever met."

"What do you mean?"

"Everyone here has an origin story. People come here for so many different reasons, leaving so many different lives behind. Even the locals. How their parents or grandparents got here, everyone's Aspen origin story is interesting. I've actually been thinking about starting like an Instagram account about this."

"How would that work?"

"Well, I'd take like a profile photo of the person, any person, could be a lifty, accountant, celebrity, whatever, and in the caption I'd write their story as to how they got here and why."

"You want, you could use me as a test run?"

"Okay stand still, I'll get a photo now so that I have one."

"How are you going to write my origin story?" I asked as she snapped a photo.

"Well, you have to tell me first." And that's what I did as we walked toward Gabriel's hotel where my truck was parked. We left each other on a good note. No, a great note. I wasn't sure if after that meeting, I'd ever see her again. Too bad. She had an undeniable way about her. Bright and sunny.

* * *

Christmas came and went and all of sudden it's Friday December 26th. Tomorrow, my story would be published. The snow polo event was where I needed to be this weekend after skiing with Marcia and Francisca. I knew that I'd be seeing some of the characters in my story at that very event. Snow polo. I didn't even know where I was going or what I was going to see. People like Harry Garr and Ted Gaffney, I figured they'd be there.

* * *

Of course I couldn't sleep that night. I tossed and turned and got up three times for water. Then it was five in the morning and my day was about to start. The only thing I could think to calm my nerves was, oddly, reading fiction. Old Colorado could wait. I tried reading the Faulkner I was on, but I just couldn't focus. Had to do something. I decided to skin up Ajax before meeting Marcia and her sister. I wouldn't be coming back here until later, so I packed ski clothes and the nicest stuff I could find for snow polo. Lyons was going to join me after helping set up the event. Alyssa and I had yet to start talking again. It was clear we were done.

It was a strange feeling for me unlike anything I'd ever felt as a journalist. As I slowly skinned up Ajax, people in town were reading the Chung piece; online and in print. I arrived to town and parked in the garage, I drank a coffee in the lobby and saw the day's papers set out for guests. There was a stack of Aspen Heralds next to a stack of Wall Street Journals next to a stack of New York Times. The Wall Street Journal headline had something to do with holiday retail sales figures, the Times had a story about some virus spreading in China, and then there was the Herald. I don't like thinking of titles for my work so I let Norman write one for me.

Inside Aspen's illicit tobacco trade involving Bledsoe, Westcott Foundation, other prominent residents

By: Meko Torrez.

A 'z'! I couldn't believe it. They made the mistake again. The cover photo was one I'd taken of the warehouse in the Aspen Business Centre putatively used for storage. It was seven in the morning and guests were starting to surface for their coffee and breakfasts. I was curious to watch as they grabbed for the papers. But I didn't stay for long. I took a copy for my own records, stuffed it in my backpack and left. I had a mountain to skin up.

There was snow fall forecasted and by the time I got to the top of the Little Nell chairlift, snowflakes had already started falling. There were a few other early morning risers on their skins like me but it felt like I had the mountain to myself. My lack of sleep and food made the ascent difficult. On two different occasions my binding need adjusting. My boots felt as if the liners had worn out overnight. My sixth toe throbbed. I neglected to put water in my pack and by the time I got to the base of lift 3, I was parched and exhausted. I took a break for a few minutes to gather steam for the second half. It was just past eight and a group of two were about to pass me on their way up. When they arrived to where I was standing, they stopped for their own break. A young couple, about my age and they looked like they meant business.

The girl: "Training for Grand Traverse?"

"Grand what?"

"The ski mo race at the end of March, you from here?"

"Yeah, this is my first season here. How's it work?"

"In teams of two, racers tour from Crested Butte through the Elk Mountains to Aspen. Forty miles."

"No kiddin' sounds intense."

"Yeah, you should find a partner!"

"Know of anyone? I just moved here and don't know too many other backcountry people. I'm Meko by the way."

The boyfriend: "Meko? From the paper? We just read a story by someone with the same...that you?"

"It is."

"Is that true?"

"My story? Yeah."

"Holy shit. We had no idea."

"I thought everyone knew!"

"We just moved here ourselves, I'm Amy, this is Nathan."

"From?"

"Tahoe area, we're coaches with the ski club here," Amy said. "Only in Aspen could a story like that be front page and not some April fool's joke."

"That's what I was thinking!"

"We're actually from Upstate New York, and had been coaching out at Sugarbowl the last two seasons. We both can't believe some of the headlines here."

"That's exactly how I felt when I moved here."

"Like you say in your story, this scheme has been going on for like twenty years, and people were just fine with it."

"Yep."

"It's like our neighbour was saying the other day, there's a lot of life in these hills. We live on a mini acreage on the way to Snowmass, the guy has lived there for the past fifty years." We chatted some more before they left. They were in much better shape than I was and powered up the rest of the way.

It struck me then that there was the distinct possibility that my story could very well be brushed off by town as nothing out of the ordinary. The tourists, what did they care about what was going on in the world of Aspen locals? Prominent people involved in a cover up would probably cause a stir, however brief, during après. But tomorrow, there would be a new headline and same for the next day. The amount of news sources at our finger tips nowadays, what chance did my little story have of any lasting impact?

If nothing else, all I may have done was piss a few powerful people off in town and nothing more. Would law enforcement actually do anything about the whole mess? Where I stood, halfway up a mountain at quarter past eight in the morning, I was thinking maybe not. It took two newcomers in Nathan and Amy with a similar sense of the ridiculous for my story to resonate. But then they were off in their own world doing their thing and just like that, my story no longer had any piece of their mindshare. It was a depressing realization. But maybe it was just the lack of sleep and food and strain my body was under after walking up to where I stood. Hard to say, so I put my head down and continued my trek upward. As I made my final push to the top, Nathan and Amy zoomed by and waved.

In the summit lodge, I opened the paper on a table, sat down, and gave it a good, close read. It was difficult for me to read my own stuff in print and not think that every other word was wrong. This time though, I was content with what I'd written. Norman is a good editor and made my writing much better than what I'd sent. The things he cut, while I thought important and entertaining, he had a point. The photos were captioned well and it was cool to see my eight thousand word piece take up two-thirds of the entire issue. When I finished, I folded it up and reassembled my backpack. I noticed that there weren't any Heralds around. I left my copy splayed out on the most central table hoping for it to be read by as many skiers as possible.

Outside, I put my skis on and took a moment to look around as snow fell from the sky. I was tired, sweaty and hungry. I grabbed my poles on the snow beside me and pushed. And then before I knew it, I was hurtling myself down the mountain. I was skiing down to the town of Aspen where a new reality awaited. I wanted to get down as soon as possible and reenter the world. My relationship to the town had changed. To what degree, I had no clue.

* * *

At the bottom, of course there was no immediate stampede of people asking me questions about the story. Perhaps for one split second while skiing down I thought that may happen. How silly. I still had twenty minutes before my time with Marcia and Francisca. I went back to Gabriel's hotel and had a big breakfast. Everyone in there must've been wondering whether I was actually a guest. Since starting this gig, I'd been asked a few times by staff how I was connected with the hotel and why my truck was always in the parking garage. I had only to say I was with Gabriel Coutinho and immediately I was treated like a high roller.

As I finished breakfast, Marcia, her sister and father appeared. Gabriel was holding a copy of the Herald, pointing at the front page and smiling while waiting for his coffee. The girls came over to where I was seated and asked if that Meko was the same one that was their instructor. I said it was. Francisca asked what illicit meant while Marcia asked about the guy I had my altercation with at Bonnie's. Yes, I told her. Same guy in the story. She read the whole thing and I think understood every part of it. Gabriel walked over and sat down across from me.

"Ana went out for a run this morning and brought back a copy. She had no idea you were a writer and I think she has a crush on you now," Gabriel said laughing.

"Lucky me."

"Don't get any ideas, I can't go through another break-up right now."

"I can relate."

"You want to write about some crazy shit? Come down to Rio."

I left my backpack in my truck along with my phone and everything that was electronic. I wanted a day on the mountain without phone calls, emails, music, anything. I wanted to get back to the basics of teaching skiing. How to get from point A at a higher elevation to point B at a lower elevation. Smoothly, comfortably. Francisca asked if we could ski the public ski racing course again and I said sure but only two runs. The rest of the day would be my choosing. We were going to make some progress today. My time with them was now limited. They agreed and off we went skiing.

There was a long line to board the gondola. It was a powder day. The skiers joining us in our gondola cabin brought up the day's paper held in another's hand. Marcia was about to tell the lady that the author of the story she was talking about was in this very cabin but I looked at her and said with my eyes to not say a word. They were from the east with second homes in Aspen. Commenting on my story, one of them said: about time. Another said the writing needed work. Marcia giggled. The third said she hoped the perpetrators were taken to court. Three quarters of the way up, their conversation switched to dinner reservations. I'd just witnessed the life-cycle of my story.

* * *

Snow polo was gaudy, boozy, wild and excessive. The polo riders were all from places like Argentina and Spain and actually modelled for Ralph Lauren. Of course they did. Men and women on horses batted around what looked like a dodge ball. No one paid much attention to the action on the snow covered football field. Everyone in attendance was there because they paid the four figure ticket price. Except me and Lyons of course. I was shocked to see copies of the Herald strewn everywhere.

My story was the talk of the event. Maybe even of town. No one knew the author was in their presence. It was strange. Lyons wanted to introduce me to people that way but I said no. She did anyway. Society gals and old rich guys. Drinking fancy cocktails and eating lobster this, calamari that. Everyone was dressed like Aspen meets Keeneland. Of the hundred people there, it took an hour for the majority of them by word of mouth to realize I was in there. I was there to work of course, to get photos of the polo players in action and of important people partying. No sign of Alyssa. They all wanted photos with me. A well dressed guy with a beard and a Panama hat said my writing was what this town needs. I blushed and said thanks. Weren't some of these people friends with the people I threw under the bus? And then I saw Garr. He walked in with people I'd never seen. I saw him before he saw me and I took a long deep breath. It was like he knew I was there the way his eyes were darting around the crowd. I walked in front of him to make his search easy.

"Motherfucker," he said.

"Hey Harry." That's the last thing I remember.

I woke up hours later in Lyons' place with a bandage across my head and a throbbing headache. Lyons was seated next to me with a cup of tea. I asked her what happened.

"Harry was already drunk when he got there. Probably coked up too. Well, he had a broken bottle and just as you went to set your drink down, after he called you a motherfucker, he charged you and smashed you over the head."

"You're kidding," I said, feeling my wounds. Tonight, I was his Columbian Sharp-Tailed Grouse.

"Nope. Cops never came because Bledsoe ordered them not to."

"How'd I get here?"

"Well, that guy with the Panama hat, turned out he's a doctor from Denver. The security guards pulled Harry off you and threw him out. You were unconscious but the doctor used first aid to clean the cut on your forehead and wrap it up."

"What time is it?"

"Almost eight."

"In the morning?"

Lyons laughed. "No, at night. I only got you home like an hour and a half ago!" It felt like I'd been out cold all night. I really did think it was the following morning.

"Here drink this," she said. "I put some indica tincture in it. It'll help." I thanked her, took a sip and almost burned my tongue it was so hot. I was in her bed and she was still dressed like Keeneland meets Aspen.

"Meko you should just rest here for the night. I really want to stay and make sure you're all right but I have a friend's birthday to go to. I'm really sorry."

"No. Go. I'm fine. Where's Garr then?"

"Don't know. He was thrown out and then he and his buddies just took off in their truck."

"Damn. Dude's like eighty. I wonder if he's still looking for me? He doesn't know where you live does he?"

"Ha! No. I don't think anyone knows you're here. Go to sleep. You need to rest."

Lyons left the bedroom. And then I heard the front door close. Off she went to the birthday party and here I was with a throbbing headache and no real idea of what had just happened. I felt around for my phone. There was six missed calls and sixteen unread messages. The most recent was from Alyssa. She wanted to know if I was okay. She somehow found out what happened. The next one down was from Norman. He wanted me to call him "ASAP." I put the phone down and closed my eyes. Not yet. Maybe after the indica took effect.

When I opened my eyes again it was half past midnight. I called for Lyons. Nothing. I got up from the bed, my head still throbbing. I felt disoriented and confused as to what I should do next. But I had energy. I knew what I had to do. I had to find Garr. I know, stupid. But I couldn't let that old fuck get away with assaulting me. A cheap shot no less! Coward. No Torres would let that slide. No way.

"Whoah, hold on. You're not going anywhere," Lyons said. I couldn't make out where she was in the dark. I had just stepped out from her house chock full of adrenaline. She was just arriving from her night out.

"Where do you think you're going," she said appearing underneath a porch light.

"I need to go find Garr and have a little talk with him." I was trying to sound happy-go-lucky. Trying to conceal my anger.

"Uh-huh. You go back inside to bed. You can't go out like this. No way."

"Lyons please. I can't let him do this to me and think he can have the last laugh."

"Meko. Get back in the house. This is no time for you to act like a complete idiot."

I kept walking. And then she stood in my way. If I were to continue, I'd have to go through her.

"Just go back inside. This is not the smart thing to do. Go back inside. Go."

My male ego wouldn't hear it. I kept walking, right on by where Lyons stood. She was dead sober. Probably didn't imbibe to better take care of me. She had gone to a friend's birthday because that person was a friend. Made a promise. But she also had taken it upon herself to look after me, preventing her from a fun night out. These thoughts crossed my mind as she began to curse me. I was walking into trouble and I wasn't in any way showing her respect for what she had done for me. I stopped. Turned around.

"I'm sorry," I said. "You're right." I walked back to where Lyons stood and we hugged. Tears filled my eyes. She led me back into her apartment and to her bedroom. I felt exhausted as soon as I got back to her room. I made the right call by listening to her. Women are more rational than men. I fell asleep hard before she even made it into the bed next to me. I was out for the count. Like someone had given me a blow to the head.

* * *

There was no skiing for me the next day. Nor would I be attending day two of the snow polo extravaganza. I had my photos, I had my story. Nine hundred bucks I was forgoing by choosing not to ski with the girls. I messaged Gabriel saying I wasn't feeling well. He got back to me asking how my head was. He too had heard. I left Lyons' place around ten in the morning after coffee and toast. She had bread. I went to where my truck was parked in the garage. I was worried about Marcia and Francisca and I wasn't exactly sure why. It was like I had taken it upon myself to be their caretaker and today I was failing them. In my truck, I called Norman. No answer. I drove down valley and was passing El Jebel when he called back. I pulled over to the side of the road.

Norman asked, "You okay?"

"Yeah, I'll be fine."

"You go to the hospital?"

"No."

"Do you have insurance?"

"No."

"Meko, come on."

"Norman, not right now. I know."

"Get yourself some damn insurance." I felt like asking him to pay me more but I held my tongue. Not the time to be a smart ass.

I asked, "Can you fill me in?"

"No one knows where Garr is or Bledsoe. Chung is in Korea as you know and Ted has been giving statements to various news outlets across the country. Your story went national, Meko. I had the AP call me asking for permission to distribute and before they could even finish their sentence I told them yes. Hope you don't mind."

"Wow."

"Yeah. NPR called, they want you to go on Fresh Air. Meko this thing is blowing up."

"So where does that leave people like Erikson?"

"What I heard, is he is now saying he was arms length the whole time and since he's now working down in New Mexico he's absolved. That's what his lawyers are saying anyway."

"Huh?"

"Don't ask."

"And Bledsoe?"

"MIA. Same with Garr. Wouldn't be surprised though if they were to come looking for you or have people do that for them. They're not happy."

"Garr got me pretty good last night. To think, there was a time when I was drinking mezcal with him at his house."

"Things change. You feeling all right?"

"I'll be okay. You think people are looking for me?"

"Think that is a good guess."

"How about you? You gonna be okay? Still have a job?"

"Looks like we're gonna lose some advertisers, but having this story picked up by the wires, I think my job is safe. Who knows though. When can you talk to media?"

"I mean I guess I should be ready now while the irons hot, right?"

"Hate to say it but yes, I think that's the smart move. I have some painkillers if you need."

"Nah, I'll be okay. All right, well I guess you can start giving out my number."

"Thanks Meko. You still manage to get a story about snow polo?"

I grinned. This job, it never sleeps.

"Yeah. I'll send you something tomorrow morning."

"Take care Meko. Oh and by the way...your work...it did enough talking. You never needed me to open any doors."

At the horse farm, I typed up the snow polo story, made some pancakes, drank more coffee, went for a walk. Sopris looked majestic in the afternoon light. Fresh snow on the twin peaks with a cerulean backdrop. There was a mountain to summit. Would have to wait though. I felt dozy around mid-afternoon and went to lie down on my living room couch. Donna was traipsing around upstairs with the radio on. I sent her a message to keep it down and then closed my eyes. When I opened them, it was eleven at night. I closed them again and slept through the night without trouble. My body needed rest to heal the blunt force blow to my head. I didn't think it was that bad but my body was telling me otherwise.

I laid low until New Year's Eve. Gabriel understood. I told him I thought it better than to go out in public right now. Not to mention how busy I was interviewing with all sorts of different media people. It was draining. The common denominator between them all, and I talked to seven different media outlets, one even from Canada, was they couldn't believe this had been going on for so long. I told them it took an outsider to have the balls, for lack of a better phrase, to collect enough material and to decide to write it. But in actual fact it also took balls to publish it. Thanks to Norman and his boss to give the okay. It also took Chung making the mistake of breaking into the wrong house to set this whole chain of events off. And the fluke of Stan remembering Darwin Hamilton. There was lots of luck involved.

Chrissy Matthews from the New York Times called on the last day of the year. She called around four in the afternoon, six o'clock on the east coast. I asked her why she was working on New Year's and she said she worked for the Times, work never sleeps. We talked for a long time. She was the only one who wanted to know more about the connection the scheme had to ferreting out information about the more serious stuff. I wished I could tell her more about that end of the story, but all I could tell her was what Ted had said to me on his porch. I told her Ted said the scheme was a crucial cog in the machine to combat narcotics entering stateside from Mexico. She said she knew. This was her beat. Chrissy gave me plenty more information about Ted's history defending but also prosecuting drug traffickers. I was embarrassed at having no knowledge of what she was saying. I even said I was sorry, to which she said not to worry. She'd been writing about this subject for the past five plus years. She said that with my exposé, there was a good chance that a guy like Ted would be in trouble. The federal government couldn't let this get out of hand, a story about a Colorado cover up. The government, for no other reason than optics, would have to do something. That's what Chrissy thought, anyway.

I asked her blankly if she thought I did the right thing, the way I structured the story, how I chose to even do the story. I felt an immediate trust in her judgement. She was from the big leagues. She knew what was going on. She laughed. "You're working on a novel right now aren't you?"

"How'd you know?"

"It's in your prose."

"That obvious?"

"It's okay, I thought it was well done. I could never do that kind of thing."

"Thanks."

"But I bet you've thought about one day writing for magazines or maybe even the Times?"

"Yup."

"I was where you were ten years ago."

"So did I do the right thing?"

"You know the answer, I don't need to tell you. But what I will tell you is that these guys are probably going to tune you up a little if they haven't already. No free lunches."

"I'll send you a selfie. I got a nice gash on the right side of my forehead."

"That's it?"

"So far."

"These guys aren't done. You going out tonight?"

"It's New Year's. Yeah."

"They'll be out looking for you."

"How about you. You going out?"

"I live in Manhattan. It's New Year's."

"Don't work too hard."

"If you're ever in the east, let me know." Chrissy hung up. My headache was gone. I was smiling. I didn't need Aspen anymore. I liked it here, loved the skiing, the music, the small town vibe, but my blind ambition toward my career won out. I now had an in with the Times! Not only that, I had a night out ahead of me. New Year's Eve for chrissake.

* * *

Gabriel was the mastermind for the evening festivities. I was to drive to his place and then concierge would drive all five of us, Gabriel, Ana, Marcia and Francisca up Castle Creek road to the backside of Ajax. People lived back there, up Midnight Mine road to Little Annie. It was another community. Old Aspen. Gabriel's LA friend had a friend who had a place up Little Annie. The plan was to have food and drink at the house and from there, snowmobile with our ski gear to the top of Ajax to watch the town's fireworks. Ten o'clock at night. And then ski down the frontside to a big Gatsby-esque house party at the base of the 1A lift. Everyone would be there. Lyons even said she and her friends would show. For a bit, anyway, before going to a party for the young and broke. People like me. I was fine with it all. I wanted to have fun. This whole episode had drained me. I wanted fun, I needed fun. Would some of the characters in my story be at Gatsby's house? Likely.

* * *

Up Little Annie's, we found the house and went inside. There were plenty of people. The food was exceptional. The guy who owned the place, he made his fortune apparently in construction. To me, the term "construction" another way to say: don't ask. We drank, we ate and then we got on the snowmobiles to buzz our way up to the top of the mountain. I was having a great time, so was Gabriel, so was Ana, so was Marcia and Francisca. Everyone was. People at the party were congratulating me for the story and asking if I was okay given my head wound. Where was my girlfriend, a few asked. I wasn't sure. I'd be seeing my friend Lyons later at the party, probably Alyssa and Eve too. Aspen's small. We got to the top of the mountain just as the fireworks went off. My arms were tired from holding a water ski rope behind a snowmobile with my skis on. There were hordes of people on the mountain drinking, celebrating, watching the fireworks. Did I really want to leave Aspen?

We skied down the frontside over to Gatsby's. A big house. Massive. Ski-in/ski-out. How some people live. By the time we got there, the party was in full motion toward the final moments of this eventful year. What would next year bring? No use thinking about it. I was here, in the moment. Perhaps my best entrance to a party ever. We came in with our ski gear and changed into our New Year's clothes in the front door hallway. Expensive paintings hung all over the place, a private catering service taking care of coats, food, drinks. A valet service. Long ways from Arroyo Seco. We didn't have a car to park. We had skis to lean on a wall.

I was milling around, eating, talking, laughing when I saw Norman across the room. Didn't think he'd be at a party like this. Don't know why I thought that. I went over to where he was and he greeted me not with a smile but with a concerned look. He grabbed my arm and said he needed to have a word. We went outside among cigarette smokers. Norman cut to the chase.

"Meko, you should get of out town. I tried to call you, no answer. Where's your phone?" I patted myself, realizing then I'd forgotten it in my truck.

"Why? Life's good! Look at this party, look at how the story went for us. I was on the phone today with the Times! Chrissy, her name—"

"Meko, you gotta get out of here." Norman was serious.

"These guys, they aren't guys whose shit list you want to be on. We're talking Sinaloa—"

"Norman come on. Level with me. What's different now compared to a couple days ago?"

"I'll tell you what if you just listen!"

"All right, I'm listening." I really was.

"I got a call today from an unidentified number. The guy on the other line had one of those things that makes your voice sound deep and robotic."

"Okay?"

"Anyway, they know where you live, they know what girls you've been sleeping with. They said as much over the phone. To me."

"They called you? Why not me?"

"Meko, I have no fucking idea. Bottom line is, they wanted to know where you were and all I could tell them was I wasn't sure."

"These guys are bad news?"

"No idea. Could be a prank for all I know, But I do think you should get out of town for a while. Let this storm blow over."

"You really think so?"

"I do. What's there to gain if you stay?"

"Well, my pride will still be there."

"Goddamnit Meko. Get over yourself. You want to get hurt? How about those girls you've been with. You want to put them in harms way?" Norman had a point.

"Where do I go? When?"

"Where is up to you. When, as soon as possible. Meko, I'm sorry. This isn't what you want to be hearing on New Year's Eve, but you gotta get out of here."

I left Norman standing there. I said thanks, that I'd consider it. At least Norman could say to himself, it wasn't because he didn't try. Was I going to leave? I didn't want to. How bad could these guys really be? I didn't want to start thinking I was living in some airport thriller novel. That's just not how life works. I went inside the party and there I found Lyons and her friends. It was eleven thirty and they wanted to go to the other party. The young and broke party. I went with them.

It was more my style. Young people, drinking cheap booze, listening to vinyl, dancing, laughing. This was a party. When the clock struck midnight, I had a good long make out with Lyons. Felt great. We were dancing. People were doing their share of cocaine. Not me, but I could understand it. This was Aspen after all, on New Year's. I was outside taking a piss in the snow when I saw an SUV slowly drive by. I wasn't hammered but I wasn't sober. I didn't think anything more of it and went back inside the house. I looked over my shoulder, there was nothing to look at it.

Lyons saw a look on my face that prompted her to ask if there was something wrong. I said there wasn't and grabbed her hand to go dance on the shag carpet. It was a danceable song and we danced. I was doing my best to not make myself look like a fool. She of course was smooth as a baby's bottom moving to the beat. I twirled her around a few times, did some faux fox trotting. I was in the groove, New Year's in Aspen. But then I saw her, across the room in the kitchen. Alyssa. She was staring right at me. I turned away but then inevitably turned again to face her. This time, she was looking at me and pointing. As she was pointing she was saying something to someone I couldn't see. Why was she pointing and who was she talking to? Was Garr here? I hoped so. Maybe it was Bledsoe. Or maybe it was her pointing me out to a friend of hers. Impossible for me to know.

It became clear, real quick though when, emerging from the shadows of the kitchen, two guys wearing black everything started walking toward me. One was bald, the other had a black ski hat on. They looked like they wanted to chat. I told Lyons to hang on a minute, that I'd be back soon. I walked over to the kitchen and one of the guys grabbed my right bicep. He dragged me out of the house before I could say anything. Alyssa led the two guys, both of which now had a grip on me down the street. I started yelling, but it was useless given the party atmosphere enveloping the neighbourhood. One of the guys smashed my throat and said to keep quiet. The other asked Alyssa what they should do once they got to the SUV. The SUV. It was the same one that drove by me while I was taking a leak. Not only that, it was the same one that came by to pick up Alyssa at Garr's in November. To think, it was Alyssa in there pointing me out. They spoke Spanish to each other. We got to the car and when Alyssa ordered the guy on my right to open the door, I kicked him in the balls. He went down hard.

And then I elbowed the other guy in the throat as hard as I could. The guy I kicked was on the ground writhing in pain. The other guy was gasping for air but he stayed up. Tough son of a bitch. He put me in a head lock. Threw a bag over my head. Threw me in the trunk of the car. It peeled off. I couldn't see anything. Pitch black. We traveled fast. I'm in a bad spot. But then the car smashed on the breaks. I heard voices. Rapid fire Spanish. High pitched. Wait a second. I recognize that voice. The trunk flings open. I'm thrown onto the street. The bag is ripped off my head. I look around dazed, confused. There's another car blocking the road, its doors are open. There's another fight happening. I stand. They don't see me. I can hardly make out what's happening. And then I hear my name being yelled.

"Meko! Correr! Sal de aquí ahora!"

Yasiel.

I had a five second window to get out of the situation. Alyssa came over to where I stood. I looked into her eyes. For a brief second, she looked sorry. Maybe that's what I wanted to see, I don't know. Her look turned to ice. She didn't say a thing. I turned and ran. Didn't look back. Yasiel and someone else, Don I assumed, there for me. I suppose Alyssa could've done something, anything, to prevent me from running away. She didn't. Was that her doing me a favour? I don't know. Alyssa, there's a girl that until the day I see her again, will completely and utterly confound me.

I ran back to the house and grabbed Lyons by the arm. I told her I had to go, that there were guys outside trying to kidnap me. She thought I was kidding at first but then she saw the fear in my eyes. She asked if she should come with me, and I told her to stay and hide herself among the partygoers. That I would call her soon to let her know what was going on. I kissed her again, a good long kiss, and then I made a run for it. My truck was at Gabriel's. I had to run to town and grab it and my ski gear from Gatsby's if I wanted to see my skis and boots and poles again. I did, so I went there after I got my truck. Gatsby's had died down. There were a few people still laughing it up, but I didn't stay for more than a few minutes to say my thanks. I found my gear in the garage and left without a trace. I never said goodbye to the Coutinho's. They weren't there anymore anyway. It saddened me to not see them again before this most unplanned departure. Such is life.

At this point, I had one thing on my mind and that was to get out of Aspen. Time to go. Norman was right. I threw all my gear in the pickup and saw the time on the dash. Two in the morning. As I drove down valley, my mind raced with questions. Do I stay at the horse farm for a while? They, whoever they were, knew that's where I lived. Alyssa knew. Do I pack all my belongings up and move out? Not enough time. Grab the essentials, get out of there. I had yet to be paid by Gabriel for my services, but I knew he would come through. Still, I only had a few hundred in the bank. I had to get out of town. I would call Donna, Norman, everyone in the morning to explain.

At the horse farm, there was an SUV high centred on a snow bank leading up to the house. Headlights shooting off into the night sky, engine still running. What had happened? I jumped out of my truck and went to look. The windshield was smashed and dead in the front were two Hispanics I'd never seen before. Gun shot wounds. Blood everywhere. Complete mess. Whoever was after me had already tried to find me here. I ran to my truck and drove to the house. Roger was at the front door with his shotgun. "Easier than the mountain lion," he said.

"Roger, what happened?"

"I knew something was up soon as I saw that vehicle. They were parked there and I came out with my gun and soon as they saw me, buddy rolled down the window and pointed a revolver at me. Well, I got 'em both before they even had a chance to say Happy New Year's."

"You're kiddin! You okay?"

"Oh I'm fine. Them, not so much."

"How'd they get—"

"Up on the bank? Buddy floored it when he got hit."

I couldn't believe this was all happening. I explained my situation to Roger and left him there. Donna wasn't home. I tore my place apart gathering necessities. Computer, clothes, some food, really not that much. I was only now just starting to feel a part of crazy old Aspen. Eve was right, my origin story here, unlike most people's. And my exit. I packed my truck up. It took no more than forty-five minutes. I downed a gallon of water hoping it would sober me up. I figured the people out to get me, they would be looking for my truck on the eighty-two west toward Glenwood Springs. What were my options? I couldn't go east over Independence Pass. It was still closed. The last way out of the Roaring Fork Valley was McClure Pass. So that's where I went. I hauled ass. Not so fast that I'd get pulled over by the cops, but fast enough. I would fail a Breathalyzer undoubtedly. Couldn't get stopped.

To the east, Sopris loomed. The stars were out and the moonlit mountain cascaded above. I looked at it a good long while as I drove without radio. The mountain's ridgelines cut into the night sky with quiet ferocity. The mountain loomed over me; haunting. I couldn't look at it any longer. Never before had I been forced to leave a place. There was still so much I wanted to do here. Would I be back? Not any time soon. Could be years. Would I see Lyons again? Eve? Alyssa? Did Alyssa even know what kind of trouble she was mixed up with? Would these assholes go after Lyons, Norman, Eve in lieu of not finding me? Did they know where mom was? I couldn't let all these questions get the better of me. I just had to drive, keep driving.

* * *

At four in the morning, I got to Paonia on the west side of McClure Pass. I could barely keep my eyes open. I filled up at a gas station and drank a couple of energy shooters. Had to keep going. In the predawn light. From the north there was a cold wind. Was it a tell to drive south? I took it as a cue. An old crow was perched on a stop sign as I turned left onto the highway from the station. It had a gnarled look. It was old. In my sleep deprived state, I figured, must be the oldest in the county. The old crow flew off into the wind when I rolled my window down to get a better look. The bird was flying south and so would I.

Back to Arroyo Seco? Too easy. Had to go somewhere else. Where that was, an open question. I drove well into the morning and despair overtook me. What was I doing? Why had I risked my life, and those I cared for all so that I could further my own career? How selfish! I felt sick. Eventually those negative thoughts bottomed out. I hit rock bottom from my own internal crisis as I drove into Ouray. I had to stop for more coffee and by now cafe's were open. Could I just stay here? I suppose I could. But fear drove me out of that little mountain town. I couldn't risk it. I had no clue what they would've done to me had I not made my escape. Did that only just happen less than eight hours ago? It was all so surreal. I kept driving. Turned the radio on. Jumped around a bit to find a good station. I almost drove off the rode when I heard whose show it was. It was Carlos, playing Blake Mills. And just like that, I was then able to force the negativity out of my head. All the unanswerable questions. I was able to search for something positive to think about on my mind's clean slate. Something to propel me forward on my drive south.

What could it be? Not women. No, too raw right now. Not my career as a journalist or the thought of skiing down a slope. What left was there for me to think long and hard about? Lots, of course, but really there was only one thing. When I thought of it, I knew it would take me to where I needed to go. I grinned. I couldn't help it. I could spend hours inside my head thinking about this very thing.

Old Colorado.

Epilogue

It's been a few months since I saddled up, hauled ass out of Aspen. Considering the state of the world, and I where now find myself, no harm in going back to my daily ritual of journaling. Lots has happened since my narrow escape from the Roaring Fork Valley. I ended up driving as far south as Big Bend on the Texas-Mexico border. Ruminating over my forced departure among the Chisos Mountains, Texas madrone and Arizona cypress. Waking each morning to the song of Santa Elena canyon wren. I camped for weeks on the banks of the Rio Grande; going into Terlingua whenever necessary to buy food, water, life's essentials.

My contracting the corona virus occurred on one of those trips into town. I don't know how or when but my guess is from sharing a pitcher of sangria one night at a bar with a couple Aussie girls. They were visiting from Marfa before returning to Austin and then home to Fremantle. It was the worst flu I've ever had. My sense of smell and taste, gone. I could hardly breath. It took three weeks for me to come out the other side. I had to deal with the virus in a campsite. I was never tested, but reading the news, talking to a Terlingua nurse, my symptoms were obvious of the virus that has dropped our world to its knees. Once I started feeling better by early March, my time camping was over. I needed a bed and sheets. I'd lost twenty pounds. But where to go now?

I wasn't going to return to Taos and risk passing the virus over to people like my mother. She's about to turn seventy, has asthma. She's been self-quarantining since mid February. She was ahead of the curve by a long shot on the whole social distancing thing. Big Bend eventually closed anyway to prevent people congregating and passing around the virus. Testing in the United States has been so far behind other countries that it really is hard to know how bad it is going to get here.

Gabriel sent my earned money and a generous tip. I don't have to work for a while. He asked where and how I was. When I told him, he demanded I go stay at a friend's place with the perfect self isolating set-up. I was thinking his friend in Santa Monica but no, a different friend. Up in Newport, Rhode Island. I hadn't been back to New England since Dartmouth. But I was keen to go if for no other reason than to sail. And for Folk Fest, if it happens. After driving twenty three hundred miles, Newport is where I now find myself. Self-quarantined on a forty-foot sailboat owned by Gabriel's friend Alonso. Alonso also has a big yacht, which is where he is at the moment in the Grenadines. The boat he's letting me stay in, his guest boat.

It's off-season here in Newport. It feels colder than the coldest days I had in Aspen. The winds coming off the ocean, the lack of sunlight, I long for Texas or Colorado. Spring skiing would be great right now though the resorts are all closed. The backcountry is where I am sure everyone is who won't let lift closures change their ways. From what I gather, the aftermath of my story being published is still unfolding. I'll get the occasional update from Norman about the state of affairs in town. Thankfully, he never lost his job. And of course, I read the online version of the Herald everyday. I miss Aspen.

What's happened thus far: Bledsoe was forced to step down. What he's doing now, I don't know. Nothing happened with Garr. He got off, and so did Erikson though he will never work for any Native American related institution again. No clue what Ari's up to, but through mom I did hear he was able to sell Tim's plein air series. Chung maybe got it the worst. He's stuck in a South Korean prison. His legal situation is on hold due to corona. No mention of Pete. I would imagine he's laying low around the Gulf somewhere huntin' bird. Ted Gaffney? Diane Westcott? Norman said a federal prosecutor is preparing a case with the help of the Arapaho. It could take years before going to trial.

Everything is on hold because of corona. It was maybe the best thing that could've happened to the guys behind the Syndicate. I'm sure Ted licked his lips as soon as the word pandemic popped up in the media. The upside for me is that I think it serves as a great buffer against them being indignant toward me. I am sleeping much better at the thought of this in my sailboat which gently rocks up against the dock from waves made minor by the marina. Smells of the Atlantic, seagulls squawking, there are charming qualities to this place I appreciate more with each day. I've never had fish and chips so tasty served at a nearby pub. The owner's wife is in charge of the place since he came down with the virus and is sadly in critical condition at the hospital. She just soldiers on with a takeout service of which I am a customer every single night. Sometimes lunch too. As for Don and Yasiel? Ghostly silence.

What do I do with my time? I'm almost finished Old Colorado. I don't know what I'll call it, and there is still lots of revision to be done, but I feel like I am almost there. My word count is just short of eighty thousand. To reach that number alone is for me a point of pride. Eighty thousand words! Just get the words down. I've done that. When I'm not writing, I read. When I'm not reading, I go for walks up and down Newport's boardwalk. Or drives through pastoral New England. Charming countryside so different from my wide-open western roots. Maybe I'll look up my boat building cousin.

I've already been through the throes of the virus, so I am not so concerned to be outside and in the general vicinity of others. Rhode Island's governor is urging everyone to stay at home. Non-essential businesses are boarded up. Essential business includes grocery, gas stations, liquor (oddly), and thankfully in my case, media.

The Newport Daily News, I've been reading it everyday. Newport's small like Aspen and somehow it also has two competing newspapers, both dailies. The Daily News comes across as the more independent, adventurous of the two and so it gets the majority of my attention though I read the other one just as much anyway. I told Norman about it all and he said he knew the women who helped start it. Debby Fukuyama. They went to grad school together. Of course you did, I said. He laughed. Norman said she no longer works full time but still has lots of say. She's a contributing editor and what that title actually means, I don't know. Norman did me a big favour by getting on the phone with her a few days ago to see if she could help me get some freelance work while marooned here.

In less than an hour I have a video chat with her scheduled. We're going to go over a few things about what the paper is looking for, expectations, and so forth. Two out of three of their staff reporters are down with corona and I think they could really use some help right now. Advertising is scarce. Tough times in community news. I am glad to help, free of charge. My form of pro bono. It's been a few weeks since I last heard from Chrissy at the Times. She said she'd be up in Newport with her husband for a short weekend getaway and that we could finally meet in person then. Corona got in the way however and now she's stuck in her Tribeca apartment. New York is the virus' epicentre. At least she has a husband there with her. Must be nice.

I don't have anyone to share a bed with and all my communications with Lyons and Eve have slowed to a trickle. It's too bad but I suppose it was bound to happen given the short period of time I was in Aspen. Alyssa I later found out was Harry Garr's goddaughter (mom's side). That explained a few things. There's not been a peep from her. She confounds me.

In a weird way, it's comforting knowing Aspen's a ghost town. Comforting in a sense that I'm not missing anything other than spring backcountry. There was a story in an outdoors magazine the other day about a big avalanche south of Telluride in Ophir. The writer went to pains arguing the irresponsibility of these skiers given the strain on Colorado's healthcare resources. The message: stay out of the backcountry. Makes sense.

Anyway, here I am in another rich person's town, another off-season, about to start writing for another newspaper. Wasn't I just here? It remains to be seen whether I'll choose to stay for sailing season. I do hope I can see what this town is like in full swing. I'm not the greatest sailor, but I do know how to hoist a spinnaker. My celestial navigation could use some work. Alonso said he wouldn't be back any sooner than August. I've got time to sail, write, and hopefully soon, get to know Newport's locals more intimately. Until then, I'll keep banging away on Old Colorado.

* * *

I'm lying down in the boat's stern as I write longhand. The gentle movement of seawater against her hull, hypnotic. I keep my laptop in the bow and now I hear the video chat's ringtone. Must be Debby though she's half an hour early. I grab my laptop and see it's a different name. An unexpected name. Lyons.

Acknowledgements

For your tireless help, encouragement, love and inspiration, thank you: Denise Lemaster.

For early readings, edits and feedback, thank you: Joanne Bragg, Larry Kerr, Kevin Rose, Callaghan Kerr, Tom Bernard, Amanda Rae Busch, Trevor Rose, Brad Randel, Brad Collins, Owen Enright, Justin Woodman, Greg McMahon and Jamie Levitt.

For my introduction to the Roaring Fork Valley, thank you: Mike Tache, Anda Smalls, Johno McBride, Alice Black, Patrick Hasburgh, Corey McLernon, Daniel Shaw, Erica Robbie, Lorenzo Semple III, Douglas Riboud, Erin Greenwood, Bob Braudis, Mo Mitchell, Chase Ennis, Marie Aufrere, Willie Volkhausen, Kendall Kraus, Casey Altman, JoJo Coffey, Jared Ettlinger, Rocky Kroeger, Cuyler Morris, Heather Sinclair, Caroline Tory, Jim Rose and Jack, Diego and Rocky - the Thistle Lane Lads.

About James

James grew up in British Columbia's Columbia Valley and holds a bachelor's degree in commerce from the University of Calgary. As a journalist, James has written for the *Financial Post*, *Aspen Daily News*, *Calgary Herald*, *Forecast Ski Magazine*, *Columbia Valley Pioneer*, and *BOEReport.com*. In 2018, James completed a residency in Environmental Reportage at the *Banff Centre for Literary Arts*. As an alpine ski racing coach, James has worked with *Team Panorama Ski Club* and *Aspen Valley Ski and Snowboard Club*. James co-founded *rose bros coffee* with his brother, Trevor. *Chung Piece* is James' first novel.

jamesrosewrites.com
ig: jamesrosewrites
tw: @jamesrosewrites